ᔕ ᔕ ᔕ

The sound of footsteps stopped. Only the wind and the blare of a car horn far below could be heard.

Except for the mercury vapor light at the entrance to the stairwell, the roof was dark. Tally continued to scan the shadows.

The crunch of gravel began again. Tally tried to follow the sound, but the wind sent it in all directions. Alarms were going off in her head. Quickly, she pulled her .38. "Who's there," she barked. The footsteps quickened. Still in a crouched position, Tally swung first to the left, then the right.

No answer.

Time slowed to a crawl. Suddenly, out of the darkness, a powerful arm closed around her windpipe, cutting off her air. "Drop the gun, McGinnis, or I'll snap your pretty neck, just like a match stick."

Reluctantly, Tally complied. The attacker kicked the gun aside, along with a spray of gravel. A cold, metal blade savagely caressed Tally's throat. Warm blood trickled down her neck and across her chest, staining her blouse. She tried to break free, but to no avail. Her attacker was strong and Tally was growing weak from lack of oxygen.

"Well, good evening, McGinnis."

The metallic voice echoed in her skull. Dimly, Tally recognized the voice. Her eyes began to cloud over as consciousness slipped away. Then, suddenly, the grip was loosened. She gasped for air.

"Altitude getting to you?" Marsha Cox's throaty voice crawled into Tally's consciousness, sending shivers up the P.I.'s spine.

"Cox, you bitch, if you hurt Katie, I'll...."

ᔕ ᔕ ᔕ

Other Books by Nancy Sanra

No Witnesses:
A Tally McGinnis Mystery

NO
ESCAPE

A TALLY McGINNIS MYSTERY

NANCY SANRA

No
Escape

A Tally McGinnis Mystery

Nancy Sanra

RISING
TIDE
PRESS

Rising Tide Publishers
65161 Emerald Ridge Dr.
Tucson, AZ 85739
520-888-1140

Printed in the United States on acid-free paper.

Publisher's note:
All characters, places, and situations in this book are fictitious, and
any resemblance to persons (living or dead) is purely coincidental.

Publisher's acknowledgments:
Special thanks to Edna G. for believing in us, to the feminist and gay
bookstores for being there, and to the Tucson lesbian community.

First printing: December, 1998
10 9 8 7 6 5 4 3 2 1

Sanra, Nancy 1944-
No Escape/Nancy Sanra
p.cm

ISBN 1-883061-23-7

Library of Congress Catalog Card Number 98-73140

DEDICATION

For Sherry

I can't remember a
shadow where your form
wasn't the perimeter, or a
ray of sunshine that
didn't have your smile
attached.

ACKNOWLEDGMENTS

Special thanks to Lee Boojamra and Alice Frier of Rising Tide Press. Without their dedication, extraordinary hard work, and perseverance, many young writers would be silenced. Bravo and thank you from all those voices who are yet to be heard, and from those of us who know you, please accept our admiration.

With gratitude to author Jean Stewart for believing.

Many thanks to Maggie McCrystle, Carrol Cook and Vicki, my computer brains, and to my friends. No smiles are brighter.

Special acknowledgment to Dr. Angela Tiberio for technical assistance.

Prologue

Friday, June 5
10:28 P.M.

A Pacific storm blew in across San Francisco Bay late in the evening. The rain-whipped darkness cracked with thunder, and golden flashes of lightning stole through the curtains into Melinda Morgan's bedroom. Melinda slept restlessly, awakening with a start when she heard the sound of wicker brushing against the wall.

The bedroom light flicked on at the same instant Melinda reached for her revolver in the nightstand drawer. Confusion and dismay distorted her features.

The intruder moved swiftly, slamming the drawer and catching the tips of Melinda's fingers. She screamed.

"No more nonsense," the intruder growled, pulling on a pair of latex gloves and snapping the fingers into place.

Blood dribbled from the tips of Melinda's fingers as she unconsciously raised her hand to her face. "I don't understand." Her voice was shrill and trembling.

Eyes icy, the intruder shrugged and laid a single red rose on the nightstand. Tiny droplets of rain still clung to the velvety petals.

Melinda jerked back the covers, her arms flailing wildly, her bare breasts swaying as she sprawled forward in an attempt to escape.

The intruder's powerful arms pushed her back against the mattress.

The first blow from a finely honed scalpel severed Melinda's windpipe. The blade shimmered in the light momentarily. The intruder rammed it downward, between two ribs, piercing her heart. The murderer's arm rose and fell; the blade plunged into her body again. Melinda's mouth opened in silent protest as her fingernails dug a path of revenge into the killer's left wrist, to no avail. In a matter of seconds Melinda Morgan's smoky blue eyes took on the fixed stare of death.

1

Monday, July 6
4:47 P.M.

The dinner crowd had not yet arrived at the corner deli. A dozen vacant tables still waited invitingly, each adorned with a red-and-white-checked tablecloth and a black lantern candleholder. Most of the restaurant's clientele came from a half-dozen office buildings that surrounded the Transamerica Pyramid. The dinner customers were overtime workers or a few workaholics whose offices had become their homes.

The Phoenix Detective Agency, housed on the tenth floor of a large complex just across from Jackson Square, stood in the shadow of the Pyramid. Tally McGinnis owned one-third of the agency; the remaining two-thirds was split between her partners, Cid Cameron and Katie O'Neil.

The summons to meet Rita Cruz at the restaurant had come late in the day. Tally knew only that the meeting pertained to a homicide.

In a navy skirt, red blazer, and white blouse, Rita Cruz looked like what she was—a lawyer. She was an extraordinarily handsome woman who had short, shiny black hair, soft sable eyes, and elegant features.

Tally gazed at the attorney with a pleasant, expectant expression. "The article about you in the *Chronicle* last week was quite complimentary, and well deserved, I might add." Her voice was filled with admiration.

Rita nodded, smiling. "I'm not sure I would consider the reference to 'Cutthroat Cruz' a compliment. But it was nice to get the recognition." Rita's eyes showed both candor and amusement.

Tally returned Rita's smile. "I got the impression that most prosecutors are a little fearful of your aggressiveness and thorough preparation for trial," she challenged.

Rita shook her head in resignation. "If only that were true. But I'm afraid my adversaries are equally capable." The attorney looked up and smiled as Cid Cameron joined them.

Cid sat down heavily, withdrawing a package of Virginia Slims from her blue windbreaker. She ran stubby fingers through her unruly thatch of gray hair, and the solemn expression on her pugnacious features softened as she looked appreciatively at Rita. "It's good to see you again, Rita," she said, placing a cigarette between her lips and firing up her lighter. The lighter was embellished with a miniature detective badge, a retirement gift from Tally.

The attorney folded her hands over a notepad. "How's the new job?" she asked.

Cid, who was quickly approaching her mid-fifties, had spent thirty-two proud years with the San Francisco Police Department, the last fifteen working homicide. Now, as one of the partners at the Phoenix Detective Agency, she could not admit to herself that she missed her old status. "Can't complain," she answered, her voice steady.

Rita was too well mannered to show that small talk bored her. She simply pushed a slim file folder containing information about the case toward the two women.

"There isn't much there," the attorney began, pointing at the file. "A woman, a beautiful young nurse, was murdered a little more than a month ago." Rita's brown eyes seemed to sadden as she focused on Cid. "Actually . . . just prior to your retirement; you're probably somewhat familiar with the case."

The former lieutenant studied the attorney, but gave no indication as to whether she remembered the investigation.

Rita did not wait for a reply. "The woman lived in Pacific Heights in a sprawling, three-story, Edwardian house she shared with her lover, Dr. Rebecca Toliver. She was killed in her bed, throat slashed, stabbed in the heart. The rest of the gory details you'll have to get from the police, or," she continued, shifting her attention to Tally, "your pal Harry What's-his-name in Forensics."

Tally listened, her mind absorbing every word. She had been raised in Pacific Heights. Although murder knows no boundaries, it was unusual for such a crime to take place in that old manorial area of San Francisco.

"What's your involvement?" she asked, still unclear about why Rita had summoned them to this meeting.

"Dr. Toliver is my client. She was arrested the night of Melinda's death and charged with her murder."

"On what grounds?" Tally pushed.

"The murder weapon—a scalpel, covered with Melinda's blood—was found in Dr. Toliver's car. The doctor is a pathologist at San Francisco General Hospital. She works the night shift and has no alibi. In fact, Dr. Toliver seems to have been missing from her lab at the time the murder took place."

Cid mashed her cigarette in a small glass ashtray. "Is this another cut-and-dried case in which the esteemed attorney makes a mockery of the law and gets her client off at any cost?" she asked sarcastically.

Rita shifted back in her chair, her hands forming a steeple near her lips. Her expression was tolerant. "Sounds like you're doubting my ethics. I'm a defense attorney. It's not my job to question the guilt or innocence of my clients. However, I will tell you that Dr. Toliver has expressed her innocence." Rita gazed at Cid for a moment.

"Don't they all," Cid snapped, crossing her portly legs.

Tally felt unsettled. Not only did she want this case Rita was offering, she was embarrassed by Cid's rudeness. "Cid's hungry," Tally said amiably, her green eyes playful. "Throw her a slab of raw meat and she'll settle down."

The attorney chuckled, then her voice turned serious. "There's more." Rita paused to make sure she had both Cid's and Tally's full attention. "A rose was left next to Melinda Morgan's bed. A single blood-red rose."

A flood of fearful memories inundated the three women. Just seven weeks earlier, a successful computer programmer named Cathy Dorset had been savagely murdered in Little Capitan Park. The victim had been tied between two trees, bled to death, and beaten unmercifully. The killer's marker, a single red rose, had been left at the scene.

"Marsha Cox," Tally whispered, too stunned to say more.

Cid pulled at the cellophane on her package of cigarettes. The evening seemed to grow darker. A warrant for the arrest of Marsha Cox had been issued shortly after Cathy Dorset was murdered. Although Cox disappeared before she could be arrested, evidence from her teen years and onward suggested a life of heinous crime. She had become a *cause célèbre* for the media. "Anything else at the scene to suggest a link between the Morgan case and Marsha Cox?"

Rita gave Cid a helpless look. "That's all I know. However, having been involved in the Dorset case, I found the appearance of a red rose at another crime scene more than alarming."

"No," Tally said emphatically, startling both Rita and Cid. "I'm uncomfortable with the assumption that Cox is the murderer. The rose must be a coincidence. First off, I doubt Marsha Cox is still in the United States. Remember, she is, or was, a jet-setter. When she escaped capture, she probably beat feet out of the country. And second, she's too smart to draw attention to herself knowing there's an arrest warrant for murder on her head."

Every police officer or detective has one case that lives in their gut. Tally's was the Dorset murder.

"Right," Cid muttered cynically. She threw a small ball of cellophane at Tally. "Gacy, Bundy, Dahmer: they all left the country after their first murder. C'mon Tal, get real. This is what sickos like Cox do. Hell, Mad Morticia's honing her skills. Getting better at what she does."

All three women shifted uncomfortably in their chairs at the mention of Marsha's nickname.

Her eyes frozen on Rita Cruz's finely chiseled face, Tally felt both fear and horror. She'd been unable to shake a chill of doubt in her own abilities since she had allowed Marsha to escape. She couldn't help wondering what more she could have done. Even today, Marsha's words were seared in her mind; the images she'd left were indelible.

Marsha's daredevil escape had taken Tally completely by surprise. Anchored by several climbing pitons and secured by a rope, Marsha Cox had begun to rappel slowly down the face of Little Capitan Mountain. Before slipping from view, she'd goaded

Tally by tossing her a knife, as though throwing down a gauntlet. Tally had bent and picked up the knife, flooded by conflicting thoughts and feelings as she watched Marsha skillfully continue her descent. Kneeling, Tally had wrapped her hand around the rope. She could feel Marsha's movement, feel Marsha's life tethered to the rope. As she laid the razor-sharp knife against the rope, Tally understood that Marsha's life was literally in her hands. For what seemed an eternity, Tally had debated with herself and fought her most primal instincts. Finally, with a sigh, she had put down the knife.

"No," Tally whispered, shaken by the remembered scene, "I can't believe Marsha Cox had anything to do with this murder."

Rubbing her temples as if deep in thought, Cid scooted her chair forward and rested her elbows on the table. "She's manipulative. Think, Tally." Her tone suggested that her meaning was evident. "Think about what we know of this woman: she's sociopathic, intelligent, charming, a probable serial killer . . . "

Tally's voice went flat. "It's a possibility," she conceded, "but not a likelihood. Marsha Cox is a star. *Where* she kills her victims is her stage; *how* she kills is her act. Knifing a nurse in her bedroom doesn't fit. There's no glory . . . "

Rita again shifted uneasily in her chair. "You'll take the case?"

"In a second!" Cid said, her voice filled with authority.

Tally's tall, wiry body straightened. Reaching for the case file, she nodded. "Where's your client now?"

"County jail. She was charged and bail was denied. I've got an appointment with John Plummer, deputy D.A., day after tomorrow. That's why I need you to get on this right away. I want a reduction of charges and my client released on bail. From what I've seen, the evidence is flimsy. The charge of murder one is excessive and reckless. The doctor's career is being destroyed before her guilt or innocence has been determined."

"Who's handling the case downtown?" Cid asked almost gleefully. She was back in her element and there was no hiding her joy.

Rita picked up her planner and the signature red blazer. Her chair squealed as she pushed it back from the table.

"Inspector Barnard Hampton, your old crony," she said, her voice cool and measured. "He's been less than cooperative. And as far as I know, he isn't the slightest bit interested in why a red rose was left at the scene of the murder."

"Barney's okay." Cid quickly defended him. "Little slow, but a damn fine cop. I'll talk to him first thing."

"Good." The attorney stood. "Have Katie give my secretary a call to make fee arrangements. If anything breaks, call me. Tally, you've still got my home number?"

"Yes, but hold on a minute." Tally's voice was quizzical. "This murder took place a month ago—why weren't we hired sooner? And why doesn't your client have an alibi?"

Cid nodded. Those were good questions—ones she should have asked herself. Tally's mentor smiled proudly.

Tally was a quick study. Since graduating from San Francisco State University with a degree in criminology, she had absorbed much information about the degenerate side of human nature. A desire for adventure and a deep sense of responsibility had led Tally to join the police department. Her eight years on the force were distinguished, and she'd quickly worked her way up to the rank of inspector after only three years. It was generally acknowledged that not only was she a good cop, she also was an insightful leader.

She had been raised by a wealthy, doting father—a highly successful district attorney. He had tried high-profile cases and won many convictions, but his reputation reached its zenith in the early seventies, when William Harvey, the horoscope killer, was convicted and given the death penalty. Tally's mother, an irascible socialite, would have preferred a daughter who liked more feminine pursuits. She openly disapproved of Tally's career in law enforcement, believing the profession lacked prestige. Tally's father, however, always supported her career choice, although he feared for her safety.

Tally's youthful, nonthreatening appearance belied her toughness. She was no pushover. Tally continued to look questioningly at Rita, who raised an eyebrow and sighed. "Dr. Toliver is a difficult and less-than-forthright client. She's used and discarded two attorneys so far. I just got the case yesterday." She paused.

As if reading her thoughts, Tally added, "And you believe in her innocence, even though she doesn't have an alibi."

Cid suppressed a grimace. "Even if the doc is innocent, the homicide is cold. Probability of a solution is nil."

"I agree," Tally said. "After forty-eight hours the trail is murky. Clues disappear, memories fade, even evidence is sometimes misplaced."

"I *need* something to take to the D.A." Rita's tone held weariness and desperation. "Call me when you've got something."

❏ ❏ ❏

While she waited for her roast beef sandwich, Cid sipped a Heineken. "Anything worthwhile in there?" she asked, pointing at the case file Tally was reading.

Tally looked up, her eyes pensive. "Not much. Attorney mumbo jumbo from the preliminary hearing. No forensics report, no police report. A notation in the margin about the rose." Tally pushed her chair back from the table and stood up. "If I'm lucky, I can still catch Harry at the lab."

Cid watched her for a moment and then began moving her bottle around on the table in small, slow circles. "If this murder is connected to Marsha Cox—I mean, there are parallels, and Cox knows how to cover her trail . . . "

Tally was gone before Cid finished her sentence.

2

Monday, July 6
6:05 P.M.

A brief summer downpour, which had begun twenty minutes earlier, stopped as quickly as it started. Transparent clouds of vapor flowed upward from the blacktopped street and cement sidewalks. The air smelled fresh and clean.

Tally strode briskly down Jackson Street, her thoughts in a turmoil. Her strawberry-blonde hair, cut in a short bob, swung rhythmically in time with her footsteps. Her green eyes held an intent, inward expression and more than a hint of fear. *Marsha Cox! Morticia!* The names called up a host of images and emotions as Tally mentally reviewed what she knew about the woman's life.

A few years younger than Tally's thirty-eight, Cox had spent much of her life slipping through law enforcement cracks. Raised among the nouveau riche of Nob Hill, she was safeguarded by an unwritten code of silence. The wealthy took care of their own, careful to always project a picture of impeccable behavior. In this case, however, high society had made a glaring error: Marsha Cox was the dark mistress of murder.

Marsha had inherited the Cox Funeral Home shortly after she graduated from college with a degree in mortuary science—hence her nickname, Morticia.

With her slim build, average height, and dark good looks, Marsha looked like a successful businesswoman. Although she had the American dream of money and success in the palm of her hand, Marsha had allowed it to slip through her fingers as she followed her darker inclinations into a life of crime.

The sun slipped from behind a big gray cloud, breaking Tally's train of thought as she reached the parking garage. For a few seconds she stood near the entrance and allowed the brilliant rays to touch her cheeks. Her spirits lifted.

Tally stepped inside the dim garage and diligently glanced around the enclosure; except for a half-dozen cars the garage was deserted. "PHOENIX" was stenciled in bold black letters on the concrete just above where her red BMW was parked. White light from the halogen lamps danced off the car's freshly polished finish. Pleased with the appearance of her vehicle, Tally folded her five-foot-nine-inch frame into the car and smiled when she saw the fluffy, brown bear Katie O'Neil had bought the week before. "Now," Katie had instructed in her soft Irish lilt, "the wee bear will be lookin' after you when I'm not around." Her tone, as it so often did, combined joy with seriousness.

Tally's life held few surprises, but Katie's love—coming as it had after their years as business associates—had been as surprising as it was daunting. Their sharing of a home was only six weeks old, and despite Tally's haunting memory of unsuccessful past romance, and her fear of new commitment, their deeply felt love seemed to both of them the fulfillment of a lifelong search.

As she backed the BMW out of the parking spot, she glanced at the bear again. Katie's grin came to mind, girlish and surprising, a gift of mischievous charm and flirtatious passion. Pausing a second, Tally closed her eyes and breathed deeply. The lilac scent of

Katie's hair lingered in the car and called up the image of a slim, dark-haired woman a head shorter than Tally, with fair skin and a delicately sculpted face.

Katie had arrived in America eight years earlier at the age of twenty-one. She had been raised in Dublin, the only child of a cement mason and a housewife. Both her parents had died in a house fire the year before she left Ireland.

In the lean years, it was Katie who believed in Tally and the Phoenix Detective Agency. She had been a constant conveyor of encouragement with just a few misgivings: the ever-present danger Tally faced, and the sixteen-to-eighteen-hour days that were necessary when Tally was working a case. In fact, Katie's only request when they moved in together was that they both share dinner at least three times a week, and as often as possible fall asleep in each other's arms.

Tally eased the BMW smoothly out of the garage and into traffic and, hands placed high on the wheel, sped down Montgomery and then over to Market Street. Commuter traffic had cleared out early. Mondays were like that: everyone was in a hurry to get home and try to recapture the joys or solitude of the previous weekend.

Wearily she glanced at her watch. For the fifth time in as many days she had missed dinner with Katie. Tally felt a rush of guilt. She looked at the car phone and then back at the road. Her heart seesawed. She could not make herself call and apologize. It was better to stay immersed in the hunt for a killer than it was to face the fear she felt in her heart.

Out there, somewhere, Marsha Cox is waiting, Tally forced herself to think, purposely pushing Katie from her mind. *Where is she? Is she on her own, or is someone helping her, hiding her?*

She stopped for a light at the corner of Market and Seventh. To her right was the civic center. Beyond it, the library, the imposing federal building, and city hall loomed in the setting sun.

Patrick McGinnis had died on the floor in his office at city hall, his white, crisply starched shirt stained with blood, his sensitive green eyes holding Tally's image as they clouded over. A desperate defendant, afraid of spending the rest of his life in prison, had stopped the wheels of justice the only way he knew how.

"I love you, Dad," Tally said aloud, grasping the steering wheel tightly until her knuckles turned white. "And how I miss you."

A left-turn arrow flashed green. Tally followed a blue pickup truck through the light. Seconds later she could see the concrete bulk of the Hall of Justice, grand and silent, four blocks down on the left.

A young boy carrying a skateboard suddenly darted across the street. The driver of the blue pickup slammed on his brakes; a crate in the truck bed slid forward and banged into the cab. "Stupid brat!" yelled the driver.

Tally watched the boy cross to the opposite side of the street; he was obviously shaken. He set his skateboard on the sidewalk and hurriedly pushed off with his right foot. In his haste, he lost his balance and crashed into a cement partition. Tally veered the BMW toward the curb, but the boy picked up his skateboard and dashed away, a small scrape on his cheek just beginning to seep blood. Tally flinched involuntarily, her hand moving to her own cheek. For one brief but terrible moment she remembered the pain of banging into the granite wall of the cliff at Little Capitan Park. Marsha Cox had invited Tally to rappel down the mountain with her.

"*Tell me about Cathy Dorset*," Tally had asked, hanging from the wall of the precipice.

"Her death, or the beating, or how I brought her down the mountain?" Marsha's eyes had danced with malice.

"Marsha, you hung a woman like a cross of dead flesh. That's no game. That's just inhuman. That's crazy." Desperately afraid of heights, and a novice climber, Tally had clung tightly to her ropes.

"Who's crazy here, McGinnis? You're the inexperienced featherweight. I'm not trapped, dangling on the side of the mountain like a helpless kitten. I can go back up. You can't." She had poked Tally hard with her glove. *"You're a dead woman."*

Shivering at the memory, Tally tucked both her elbows close to her side. She nosed the car back into traffic, her stomach tight as a fist. She had beaten the odds that day at Little Capitan Mountain, beaten Marsha Cox at her own game. She couldn't help but wonder whether she'd be so lucky if she encountered Marsha Cox again.

3

Monday, July 6
6:28 P.M.

A white Chevy van was parked just outside the
entrance to the back of the Hall of Justice. "San
Francisco Medical Examiner" was stenciled in bold,
black letters on the van's door, along with the city seal.
To the casual observer, it was a utility vehicle. To cops,
and to most of the staff at the Hall of Justice, it was the
meat wagon: the official transport of the dead.

As she reached the double doors leading to the
Pathology and Toxicology departments, Tally heard the
clanking of the metal cage around the elevator that took
prisoners upstairs for booking. The county jail was on
the seventh floor. She felt a sense of apprehension as
she passed through the automatic doors and moved
quickly into the hall.

The familiar foul smells of chemicals, death and
disinfectants assaulted her nostrils. The corpse that had
recently arrived in the van lay to the left in the scale
room, an attendant close by. A black body bag was
draped carelessly over an empty gurney.

Tally knew the area like the back of her hand.
Her father had often been called to the lab on weekends
when a high-profile or particularly grisly murder had
taken place. As the D.A., it had been his style to be on
top of a case from the very beginning. For years Tally

had begged to tag along with him. When she was fifteen he finally relented, insisting she sit on the lime green vinyl couch in the hall while he conducted business. She readily complied until he was out of sight, and then she was off to inspect and search every nook and cranny. The technicians were tolerant of her presence, not only because she was the district attorney's daughter, but because Tally was respectful of their space and always conducted herself in an adult manner. She knew that a Stryker saw was used to detach the cap of a skull so the brain could be removed and examined, and she had smelled the stench of burning bone and decomposing flesh before most kids her age had learned to drive. She had watched with calm intensity as livers and hearts were carefully weighed during an autopsy, and she had been quick to understand trajectory and X-ray positions.

When she was nearly seventeen, however, her intense curiosity and vivid imagination were jolted by a bit of unplanned humor. She had just stepped out of the scale room when to her left she noticed a fully clothed corpse lying on the x-ray table. When she went to inspect the dead person, she was sure she heard a deep gurgling sound coming from the body. Drawing closer, her face even paler than usual, to her immense surprise and utter horror, a napping lab technician sat up and announced sleepily, "I'm hungry." Believing the technician had miraculously returned from the dead, Tally ran trembling from the X-ray room and did not return until many years later. Patrick McGinnis never understood why his daughter would no longer accompany him to the lab.

Tally's attention was called back to the present by a voice in front of her.

"I.D.," requested a security guard, extending a hand that was missing a thumb and index finger. His arm reached across a gray metal desk strewn with papers that contained security rules and regulations.

Tally passed him her driver's license. "You must be new."

He grunted something Tally couldn't hear and handed her license back. "You got an appointment?"

"Yes," she lied, "with Chief Medical Examiner Harry Sinclaire."

The guard snatched up a phone, made a quick call, and waved her through.

Tally strode briskly down the white-walled hallway and through two sliding doors into the autopsy theater. Brown tiles covered the floors and flowed up the walls. Harry Sinclaire, dressed in surgical greens and a pale blue paper apron, was stooped over one of five porcelain autopsy tables.

His task nearly complete, Harry had removed his rubber gloves and plastic mask and was talking into a hand-held recorder. He grinned when he saw Tally, and quickly held up a finger to indicate he would be right with her.

While Harry washed at the stainless steel sink, Tally fretted silently as she stared off, past the cabinet that held surgical tools. Her eyes finally came to rest on a white bleached skull. A crack ran the length of the hollow cavity, a hole the size of a half-dollar in the back. Harry had told her long ago that the skull belonged to a nameless victim who had died from a severe blow to the head and a large-caliber gunshot wound. Her thoughts drifted to Katie, and for a brief second she questioned why she was at the lab staring death in the face, rather than sharing a pleasant dinner with someone she loved. *Maybe it's time for a change.* She continued to stare at the skull as if it held some answers before finally turning away.

The door to the large walk-in stainless steel refrigerator was slightly ajar. Using her foot, Tally nudged the door until she could see inside. Double-decker gurneys draped with white sheets greeted her. Had the noxious odor of death not been so overpowering, she might have found humor in the sight of twelve pairs of feet protruding from the sheets. But the neatly printed toe tags were a grim reminder that there was no humor in death.

Harry, who was short and stout with gray flecks in his black hair, waited for Tally to bend over to receive his generous hug. He planted a kiss on the tip of her nose, as he always did when she was a small child. He pulled at the end of his short, neatly trimmed beard, his eyes full of fatherly love.

The chief medical examiner was brisk and energetic. For more years than he could recall, he had been Tally's father's best friend, and a reliable fixture at McGinnis Christmas dinners and family barbecues.

Harry pointed back toward the table. "Another baby toe tag." He shook his head sadly. "The result of our right to keep and bear arms. Fifteen years old. Didn't even shave yet."

Tally shivered. Her yellow cotton shirt and khaki slacks weren't heavy enough to ward off the cold of the autopsy room and the chilling effect of Harry's words. He took her elbow and guided her into the hall. Moments later they stood beneath a large ceiling vent, the hum of the air-conditioning fan muffling their conversation.

"So . . . what brings you to the archives of the dead? My morbid philosophy, my charming personality, or just the need to rekindle old friendships?"

"Harry—" Tally shook her head and rolled her eyes—"you've got to get a new line." She smiled faintly, her white, even teeth sparkling in the fluorescent light. "Actually I love your morbid philosophy and charming personality and I have missed you, but I also need some help with the Melinda Morgan investigation."

Harry looked puzzled.

"I can't give you a lot of details," Tally continued gravely. "She was murdered about a month ago. Worked as a nurse at San Francisco General. Young, pretty."

"Yes!" Harry nodded his head decisively. "I'm no good with names. Facts I don't forget. Dr. Toliver was arrested for her murder."

"That's her." Tally's voice rose. "You know the doctor?"

"Very well. Good pathologist. I've worked with her on dozens of overlapping cases. She even got my tail out of a sling a time or two. She's a bit of an egotist. I think that comes with her perfectionism. But I like her." As if anticipating Tally's next question he added, "Do I think she's a murderer? No. But we live in a cruel world, so who's to say."

"What about the autopsy?"

Harry shrugged and turned his palms upward. "Come on, Tal."

Her look was searching. "Hypothetically speaking, if someone's throat was slashed and they were stabbed in the heart, how would the autopsy appear?" she asked.

"Hypothetically only," he said, trying to sound both professional and stern. "What d'ya need?" His voice was softer now.

She smiled, touching his sleeve. "Information about an autopsy similar to Melinda Morgan's." She pulled a leather-bound notepad and pen from her back pocket.

"I'll give you the highlights, Tal, best I can remember, but that's it." He looked up and down the hall and lowered his voice. "Whoever killed her knew what they were doing."

"Meaning what?" Tally asked firmly.

"Say an intruder breaks into a house and slashes his victim. If it's in the neck area, as it was in this case, I usually see two, three, maybe even five wounds. It's an outpouring of rage or fear or, hell, just plain stupidity. Most of the time a perpetrator doesn't know how to kill and he or she continues to inflict wounds until the knife or whatever sharp object is the weapon of choice hits something vital, something life ending. In this case there were only three wounds: one precise slash to the windpipe and two stab wounds to the heart. No bruising. No other cuts."

"Leading you to believe what?" Tally asked.

"The perp was familiar with human anatomy. He or she knew how to kill quickly."

"Like a doctor?"

Harry nodded. "That's an obvious choice."

"Or a mortician?" Tally asked pointedly.

Harry was silent for a moment. "I don't understand."

"Marsha Cox."

"Ah. The mad mortician. Brutalized that Dorset woman. Never caught her, did they?" He pulled at his beard, remembering the Dorset autopsy. "Yes, she definitely would fit the profile."

Tally felt a hollow fear. "Was the murderer right or left-handed?" She visualized Marsha Cox sitting at her desk in the Cox Funeral Home, saw her signing papers with her left hand.

"The only reason I remember this without checking my notes is because of their precision," Harry answered, irony in his voice. "The wounds were slightly angled from right to left, which may make the perp right-handed. But that could change based on how and where the murderer was standing. It's just a guess."

Tally's shoulders visibly relaxed. "What about prints?"

Harry shook his head. "If I remember correctly, we found traces of talc."

She cocked her head, silently questioning.

"Perp wore gloves. Probably latex surgical gloves. And probably two pair. With a single glove, if they are worn for any length of time, we sometimes get a particle, or maybe a palm, or if we're really lucky, a full print. Nothing this time."

"Doesn't look good for the doctor," she sighed.

Harry nodded, patting his shirt pocket for a package of cigarettes. "Laser picked up a few fibers; all but one looked like common cotton of the type found in sheets. The other was some type of wool. I sent it to an independent lab across the bay for further analysis. Results are probably in the file. Pink fuzz was found in her hair and pubes. Matched the blanket on her bed. Nail scrapings were rewarding. Can't remember if it was the right or left hand. Got a small piece of skin and some blood from under the broken nail of an index finger. Can't remember the blood type either, but I do know the DNA matched Toliver's."

"Holy smoke," Tally said, her voice rising sharply.

A security guard sitting at his desk down the hall from the autopsy theater glanced toward them but said nothing.

"Tal," Harry scolded, "keep it down. I also found traces of blood under the nails on her other hand. It didn't match Dr. Toliver's and it wasn't her own."

"What are you saying—that two people were present when she was murdered?" Tally asked, surprised.

Harry shrugged. "Don't know. Wasn't there. Remember, the victim was a nurse. Although it's unlikely with the precautions taken these days, the blood could have come from a patient."

"That's highly doubtful," Tally answered, leaning against the wall. "You don't remember the blood type?"

Harry's forehead furrowed. "Give me a break. I'm doing better than a dozen autopsies a week, plus the paperwork and investigations, and I've still got a cooler full of toe tags. Downsizing. Lost one full-time pathologist and five techs last month, and more cuts are yet to come. I haven't left before ten o'clock for weeks. It's in the police report. Get a copy."

Tally gently rubbed his shoulder. "I'm sorry, I shouldn't have pushed."

His face broke into a sheepish grin. "I'm just tired. Based on the location of blood at the scene and her broken nails, I'd also guess the victim's fingers were smashed in the nightstand drawer. We found a gun in the drawer. She was probably attempting to protect herself." Harry waited for a prison guard to pass them on his way to the elevator. "Probably knew her attacker. No defense wounds. No trace of a break-in."

"That's it?" Tally looked at him straight on.

"No," he answered tersely. "There was no evidence of semen or vaginal bruising. She wasn't sexually assaulted." Harry cleared his throat, his voice almost a whisper. "Alcohol screen was clean. Drug screen was another story. She was high when she died. Morphine."

"Morphine?" Tally looked stung. "She was a nurse."

Harry shrugged. "Lo and behold, the gods and goddesses of medicine are fallible. For the past four months she had worked pediatric oncology. Tough field. Not that I'm making excuses for her. Still, it's not easy to watch children die."

She grew quiet and wished they had gone to Harry's office instead of standing in the hallway. "How bad was her habit?"

Harry shrugged again. "She had some tracks between her toes. She worked hard at hiding her addiction. She had been using suppositories as well."

"That changes the whole picture. It could be a drug killing."

"Possible," Harry said, shaking his head. "Drug dealers who don't get paid are nasty. Of course, Morgan could have been stealing morphine from her patients. Little here. Little there. Just enough to stay happy. If she was into anything big time, someone would've noticed and reported her to the nursing board."

"Maybe that's why she moved to Pediatrics. Maybe a supervisor or coworker noticed a change in her work habits."

"Possible. And her young patients wouldn't complain that they hadn't received their meds. Wouldn't know better."

"Were the wounds comparable to those of Cathy Dorset?"

A grimness had settled over the hallway.

Harry glanced toward the security guard. "If you mean was she bled to death, no. Nor was she beaten. But," he continued, his face expressionless, "she was abused. Earlobes were cut off."

"What?"

"They're gone. Searched the house from top to bottom."

"But why?" Unconsciously Tally pulled on the small gold loops in her ears.

Harry cleared his throat. "Who's to say why. Fetish. Cannibalism. Souvenir."

"So senseless," Tally whispered.

"Show me a murder that isn't," Harry added grimly. "I need to get back to work. Remember," he continued, half scolding, "this was hypothetical. As I've told you in the past, I've got more than thirty years with the city. I intend to enjoy my retirement."

Tally pushed her bangs back from her forehead. Her throat felt dry. She forced herself to speak slowly and evenly. "Forensics has a sample of Marsha Cox's blood taken from the Dorset crime scene. Can you match it against the blood found under Melinda Morgan's fingernail?"

Harry's patience was growing thin. "The police already have the alleged murderer. Talk to Barney Hampton." He took several steps towards the autopsy theater and then turned back to face Tally. "Give my best to your mother when you see her."

Tally smiled. "I'll do that. You know she's very lonely these days, Harry. You could ask her to dinner."

"Dinner with Victoria? Really, Tal. Your father was my friend, but friendship only runs so deep . . . not to say I don't love your mother, but a whole evening with Miss Society . . . I don't think so. I'll stick to my toe tags." He winked. "See you soon, sweetheart."

◻ ◻ ◻

The stillness of the night and the encroaching fog left Tally feeling uneasy as she slid onto the front seat of the BMW. She had never met Melinda Morgan, never seen a picture of her, but after the events of the past few hours she felt she knew her, and so far, she didn't like the picture that was unfolding.

A green light flashing just above her car phone told her she had a message.

Cid's voice filled the car, her tone urgent. "Meet me back at the office. Eight o'clock."

Tally checked her watch: seven forty-five.

4

Monday, July 6
8:05 P.M.

Sorrowful notes from a saxophone flowed out of the entrance to Topsy's Bar and Grill. The music softened the night and, for a very few precious seconds, erased from Tally's thoughts the dark shadows left by Melinda Morgan's death.

She stood across the street, listening, watching. Tourists and city dwellers crowded the street, enjoying the foggy night air. On the corner, a tall, brutish-looking man yelled for a cab, while down the street a young mother tenderly comforted a crying child. Two lovers walked by hand in hand. Katie came to mind; Tally smiled at the thought and then felt a rush of ambivalence tug at her brain.

She pulled open the glass door to the office complex that housed the Phoenix Detective Agency and quickly headed toward the elevator.

The aroma of pepperoni pizza flooded Tally's senses as she stepped into the office reception area, reminding her she hadn't eaten all day. Lights were blazing and the sound of Frank Sinatra singing "My Way" filled the room. Tally winced and moved quickly to the CD player next to Katie's mahogany desk. She replaced the moldy oldie with the smooth jazz of Shirley Horn.

A note taped to the corner of the desk had "Tal" printed in bright red letters. Katie's seldom-shown disappointment was clearly evident in her words. "You stood me up for dinner . . . again. A call would have been nice." Tally instantly felt remorseful. She continued reading, trying to justify her thoughtless behavior. "Da always said, 'It's the sharing of the harvest and the whiskey-sippin' time that blends the hearts and makes them strong.' A wee call would be good next time. Lunch tomorrow?" A hand-drawn smiley face under Katie's name told Tally she had been forgiven, but it didn't erase her own guilt.

She surveyed the room, part cop doing her rounds, part appreciative daughter. Her mother, Victoria, had taken up interior design shortly after Tally's father was murdered. The new vocation had given her mother a sense of purpose and kept her from relying too heavily on Tally.

As strong willed as her daughter, Victoria had pressed for an elegant office decor when the Phoenix Detective Agency first opened seven years earlier. Persistence finally paid off. From the pale blue brocade couch to the aquamarine wing chairs, the spacious room suggested class and quiet authority.

Satisfied that all was in order, Tally followed the tantalizing scent of pizza down the hall to Cid's office.

When Tally designed the office space, she allowed herself a couple of luxuries, as well. She made sure there was a conference room directly across from her office, and a full bath with changing room, in the event she worked late or spent the night. An office for Cid was also included, with the hope she would one day retire from the police department and come to work at the agency. It was a natural friendship, Cid the mentor, Tally the quick study. It had started fourteen years earlier when Tally took an evening class on criminal investigation that Cid was teaching at San

Francisco State University. A bond of trust and mutual respect was formed immediately, and the ties of friendship only grew stronger when Cid lost her elderly mother and Tally her father.

Her feet propped on the corner of an antique, rolltop desk that Victoria had found at an estate sale, Cid leaned back comfortably in an overstuffed, tan leather judge's chair, pizza and Budweiser in hand. Her face was furrowed, with a tiny road map of burst blood vessels that ran across her cheeks and nose, the by-product of countless glasses of scotch. She had lost fifty pounds over the last six months but, in the weeks since her retirement, had gained ten back. "Have a piece." She motioned with the beer can toward a box that had "Mama Luciano's" imprinted on the top.

"You changed your clothes," Tally observed, reaching for a napkin. "You go home?"

Cid belched loudly. "Good beer," she said without apology. "Sadie needed her taco and I needed to change my pants. Got a little barbecue sauce on them at the deli." Cid eyed her younger partner appreciatively. If the former lieutenant was happy, and more often than not she was, as she settled into her new role, it was because she felt at ease working with Tally.

Tally pulled at a piece of cheese that stretched like a taut rubber band. "Barbecue sauce? Did that come after your roast beef sandwich? You're incorrigible, Cidney, and your dog is going to roll over dead if you don't stop feeding her tacos."

"It's okay," Cid assured her. "I checked with the vet." She shrugged. "He wasn't pleased with her diet, but, hell, who else am I going to spoil? Besides, a little taco sauce and a little salsa boosts Sadie's sex appeal. She's one happy lesbian puppy."

Tally's eyes held Cid's as she tried not to smile, but she lost the battle. Making her smile was Cid's gift.

Tally felt an uncomfortable pause in the conversation. Cid seemed to be considering something; her look conveyed worry. "I saw the note from Katie. Trouble at home?"

The question surprised Tally. "Pardon?"

"Katie talks to me, Tal. She doesn't understand your behavior lately. Frankly, my friend, you're hurting her, and that isn't exactly sitting well with me. Hell, I shouldn't stick my nose where it doesn't belong, but, geez, she loves you, and I thought you loved her. The last two weeks you've found one reason or another to work late. Insignificant meetings at lunchtime, bullshit surveillance at night . . . "

Clearly the conversation was making Tally uncomfortable. "You're right, you shouldn't stick your nose where it doesn't belong." She shifted her weight from one foot to the other, sighed softly. Then in a chastened tone, "There's no problem," she added without much conviction. "You of all people should understand the obligations of this job."

"All too well, my friend. Dedication to my badge got me a whole hell of a lot, didn't it? A shithole apartment and a shaggy little dog for a companion." She did not speak for a moment. "Stop running, Tal; learn from my mistakes. It ain't fun being lonely. Katie's pure gold. Talk to her; I know she'll help with whatever's eating at you," Cid said kindly.

Stifling the urge to defend herself and anxious to change the subject, Tally quickly picked up a piece of pizza. Between ravenous bites, she updated Cid on the information gathered from Harry.

Cid lit a cigarette and inhaled deeply. "The doc looks dirty from a forensic perspective." Her words seemed hollow, her profile tense.

"Cid, you okay?"

She nodded. "I gave Hampton a call, made arrangements to meet him tonight at nine." She sounded weary. "Police found a stiff out at Little Capitan Park early this evening. Identity unknown at this point. Older woman."

Tally was silent.

"Body was naked, arms, torso, and legs spread in the shape of a cross." Smoke seeped from the corners of Cid's mouth. Her eyes were flat.

Tally's body stiffened. "I don't think we should jump to any conclusions about Marsha Cox. Don't forget the DNA match Harry found. That's powerful evidence against the doctor. And remember the unidentified blood. That could mean a second killer, could mean a drug hit. Marsha Cox is a solo act."

"Yeah, but Little Capitan is Cox's playground. Her killing field." Cid's words were raw. She pounded her cigarette out in an ashtray that was already full.

Tally thought about Little Capitan. Named after the larger peak in Yosemite Park, the thousand-foot granite mountain was surrounded by dense underbrush and evergreen and eucalyptus trees. Located only a few miles southwest of downtown San Francisco, the park was always closed to the public because of its rough terrain and the need to discourage unwanted gang activity and rogue climbers.

"Little Capitan doesn't have any barriers around it." Annoyance crept into Tally's voice. "Anyone could kill or dispose of a body out there." She paused for emphasis. "Marsha Cox is too smart, too cunning to return to the scene of an old crime. I've never seen you act like this before, Cid. It's as if you've locked your attention onto Cox and closed out everything else." Tally gazed at Cid with affection and puzzlement.

Cid's face looked older than her fifty-four years when she turned in her chair to address Tally. "The dead ain't talking, Tal. Look at the facts. Six weeks ago Cox nearly killed you. Tonight we get handed a case in which, *coincidentally*, a red rose was left at the scene.

Red roses *coincidentally* are Marsha Cox's murder marker. Then *coincidentally* Homicide gets a call about a stiff at Little Capitan." Her eyes flashed, but her voice was gentler now. "I don't want you dead. Hell, for that matter, I don't want *me* dead. Cox considers herself to be the best, the smartest, the ultimate killer. She's daring us to outwit her and catch her ass. So far, she's winning this game."

Tally ran her fingers through her strawberry-blonde bangs. She didn't want to rush to any conclusions. The picture seemed bigger than the small puzzle that was unfolding in front of her. "Maybe we need to go out to Little Capitan."

Cid shook her head. "According to Hampton, the whole park is off-limits until daybreak; the body was removed. Forensics will continue their investigation through the night and into the morning."

Tally's mind flashed back to the white van outside the Hall of Justice and the corpse in the scale room. "How was the woman in the park killed?"

"Hampton didn't elaborate. I'll see what I can find out when I meet him later."

Tally frowned. "Watch him, Cid. Barney's only interest is for himself."

"I've dealt with Barney's self-serving bullshit for years; he doesn't scare me. You, on the other hand," she said, pointing her finger, "need to watch your back. Our client, Dr. Rebecca Toliver, is in jail. For sure, *she* didn't slither through the bars and kill this woman at Little Capitan tonight."

◻◻◻

Cid's junker Plymouth Fury reluctantly climbed Grant Street, which wound up a series of graceful hills. In the distance, fog surrounded the Golden Gate Bridge, stealthily creeping ashore to drape a misty gray cloak over Fisherman's Wharf. The temperature had dropped to a chilly fifty-nine degrees. The defroster groaned and coughed before spitting out a puff of warm air.

In the silence, Cid thought about her earlier behavior. She had been short with Tally for no reason. The object of her anger, or, to be more honest, her hurt, really was Barney Hampton. It had been obvious from their conversation that he didn't want anyone from the police department to see them together. The inspector had insisted on meeting her at an out-of-the-way neighborhood bar on the corner of Grant and Chestnut. He didn't elaborate about why he had chosen the unknown hole-in-the-wall as a meeting place, but Cid guessed it had something to do with his application for promotion to lieutenant, her old position.

In the department, Barney was known as Mr. Careful. The name fit. He had a talent for political infighting, but always managed to steer clear of ruffling any feathers. When he was around the commissioner or chief, he never stepped on any toes, never made foolish mistakes. Through the years, his judicious behavior had earned him numerous friends in high places. Cid held a fondness for Barney, but he didn't fool her either. She thought of him as a weak man who was quick to delegate responsibility to his junior partner and swift with ruthless reprisal when he was crossed by anyone of the same rank or lower.

Cid's blue eyes paled under her gray, bushy eyebrows as she maneuvered the Plymouth into a parking spot. Once again she wondered if she had done the right thing by retiring from the police department. She had held a position of prominence and power. She'd been a damn fine detective. But gut instincts and good sleuthing hadn't been enough to keep the politicos from ramming a knife in her back. Cid had learned to accept, and even understand, the reasons for Barney's politicking. But she did not want to play that game. And that had cost her any further career advancement in the department.

◻ ◻ ◻

The room was a dark, paneled box. Bar stools padded with brown vinyl were lined up in front of the twelve-foot-long mahogany bar. A pool table spread its sea of green at one end of the room; a jukebox and postage-stamp dance floor held court at the other. The entire wall behind the bar was covered with autographed pictures of the Giants baseball team. Most photos were from the fifties and sixties. Willie McCovey and Willie Mays were the most prominent individual pictures, along with a current autographed photo of Barry Bonds.

Cid swung onto one of the stools. She was the only patron in the room. "Glenlivet neat," she ordered.

A short, paunchy bartender wearing a wrinkled white shirt and bright red bow tie set out an ashtray and a napkin before pouring the drink.

Cid loved her scotch. She called it her cruelty release, and used it to drown the memories of the pain humans inflicted on each other.

Inspector Barnard Hampton entered the dimly lit bar, looked around, and quickly dropped his eyes. As passionate and straightforward as he was on the job, social situations, even those connected with work, were difficult for the shy inspector. Tall and lanky, Barney was a forty-eight-year-old widower with sandy graying hair and a penchant for old tweed jackets.

"How ya doing?" Barney asked in a low, brooding voice.

Cid pulled a twenty from the pocket of her new navy Dockers and pushed it across the bar. She smiled, genuinely happy to see the inspector. "Fine, Barn. Have a drink?"

Barney sat on the stool next to Cid. Every bit of cruelty he'd witnessed during his fifteen years on the force was etched into the deep furrows on his face. He had been in the hospital twice in the past year for a bleeding ulcer. His clothes hung on his six-foot frame.

"Sorry, Lieutenant . . . ah, Cid, stomach feels like a volcano." He glanced at the bartender. "Just a club soda."

The inspector looked around, as if he were expecting someone else.

"Relax, Barney, you picked a safe spot." Cid's voice was flat, yet forgiving.

Barney stopped, eyes wide open in distress. "I shoulda known I couldn't fool you." His shoulders relaxed, and he smiled respectfully.

Cid knew he was fresh from a new crime scene, and his distrust of his own species was amplified as a result. "How are things going?" she asked.

Barney Hampton flipped his palm back and forth. "So-so. Things haven't been the same since the wife died. Kids are off at school," he continued with depressed resignation. "Gets pretty damn lonely around the house."

"Ever think of getting married again?"

His voice was bitter now. "I'm not successful in that department. Can't compete with what's out there nowadays."

Cid watched him for a moment, surprised by the anger in his voice, and then changed the subject. "Homicides up?"

"No. No increase. Five to six a month." Barney hunched forward. "It's a big load for a handful of inspectors. We need a bigger staff."

"Cutbacks are the shits, Barn. But that's part of the job. Part of the politics." Cid spread her hands in a gesture suggesting usefulness. "Maybe I can help."

"How so?" The inspector was intrigued.

"Tell me about Melinda Morgan," she prodded.

The inspector thought for a moment. He was used to yielding to her demands, but she wasn't part of the department anymore, and with a promotion close at hand, he was cautious. His brown eyes looked tired. "What's your interest?"

"Little private sleuthing for an attorney, Rita Cruz." Cid watched Barney for a reaction.

He shifted on the bar stool and glanced at the bartender, who he was sure was listening. "Regs," he finally said, puffing out his chest. "I don't need to remind you 'bout following the rules. There's nothing clearly written about working with private dicks . . . ah, private detectives. It's outta my hands. Sorry."

Cid felt a rush of irritation. "That's bullshit and you know it. The department has always worked with P.I.s. I did it for years, so have you and every other man or woman on the force. I rub your back, you rub mine. Don't recite Goddamned rules to me—remember, buddy boy, I wrote half of them." Cid's face was now beet red. "You earned the title of inspector by taking a test, Hampton, but don't Goddamned forget you earned your strips because I taught you."

"Okay, okay." Barney Hampton's face was flushed with embarrassment. He glanced at the bartender again and popped two Tums in his mouth, leaving the empty wrapper on the bar. "Don't get steamed. We'll find a way to work this out."

"Can the lecture. We share info, or fuck you, and I'll go to the chief. My guess is, he'd be damned happy to have my help."

Barney rubbed his hand across his bristly cheeks. Cid had backed him into a corner and he didn't like it. He looked carefully at his former boss, determined to save face and turn a losing situation into personal gain.

Cid was not surprised when Barney held up his hands in mock surrender. "Tit for tat and off the record?" he asked. "Anything breaks, I get it, along with the credit?" Mr. Careful looked pleased with himself.

"Of course," Cid answered shrewdly, "whatever it takes to catch the friggin' killer."

Languidly Barney pulled a black notebook from his jacket pocket and studied his notes. He eyed her directly. "Crime scene was clean as a whistle. Lotta blood, mind you, but Morgan musta gotten snuffed fast. No fight for sure. Hell, other than a few ruffled blankets, the bedroom was neat as a pin. Lamp on the nightstand was still upright. Only thing outta place was a wicker clothes basket in the hall, belonged in the laundry next to the garage. Perp musta knocked it over. Our murderer is a real neat freak. It was raining, lotta mud on the front steps, but the entry was spotless. Found a wet sponge mop in the sink in the utility room. Turns out Toliver's prints were all over it."

"That's it?" Cid demanded. "Jesus, Barney, it's Toliver's house, I'd expect to find her fingerprints on the mop."

Inspector Hampton took a long, slow sip from his glass and then quietly nodded.

"Shit, there's gotta be . . ." Cid left her sentence hanging, a frequent habit that drove Barney crazy.

The inspector rubbed his stomach as if smothering a fire. "Neighbors called 9-1-1. Front door had been standing open for more than an hour, so they tried calling the house and got the answering machine. They figured the police oughta have a look. I was called in just before midnight after patrol found the body. Toliver, the roommate, rolled in a couple hours later. Snooty dyke bitch. Thinks she's God because she's a doctor." Barney lip's tightened, emphasizing his distaste. "Looks guilty as hell."

"How so?" Cid asked, firing up a cigarette. Smoke erupted from her nose. "And, Barn, can the slurs."

He nodded as if implying he was sorry and quickly flipped a tattered page of his notepad. "Found a bloody scalpel in the back of her car. Damn thing was wrapped in a pink towel." His eyes narrowed. "Towel was part of a set in the victim's bathroom. Blood matched Morgan's."

Cid gulped half of her scotch. She was silent until the warmth hit her stomach. "I haven't met Toliver, but she's a doctor, for Christ's sake. Smart. I can't believe she'd make such a dumb—"

Barney Hampton had spent many hours with suspects and criminals; nothing surprised him. "There's more. Neighbors saw the doctor's car parked on the street when they got home from dinner at ten fifteen. Time of death was between ten and eleven. The doc hasn't got an alibi. Eight forty-five is the last time anyone at the hospital can vouch for Toliver until well after the victim was murdered."

Cid looked down at her hands; when she spoke, her voice was strained. "Damn, I was so sure that Marsha Cox was somehow involved in this."

Barney set his notepad on the bar while he searched through the pockets of his tweed jacket. "I'd guess she is, maybe in cahoots with the doctor," he said, opening a new package of Tums and popping two into his mouth.

Through her disbelief, Cid felt the hairs on the back of her neck rise. "What?"

Barney smiled faintly. It wasn't often he was a step ahead of Cid. "You know about the rose?" He didn't wait for an answer. "Coupla days after Morgan was waxed, I read the forensics report. Skin and blood were found under Morgan's fingernails. The night we arrested Dr. Toliver she had a fresh scrape on her right arm. It was three, maybe four inches long. Nasty. The DNA was a perfect match to Toliver. But get this, Melinda Morgan also had blood under her right pinky: blood type A. The doctor's blood is O positive. I kept seeing the rose in my mind. So I played a hunch. Pulled Cox's file. Bingo! She's type A all right. I called Carol Vincovich over at Forensics and asked her to run a cross match on Morgan's and Marsha Cox's blood. Turned out to be a fat zero. Cox's blood sample was misplaced, lost. Vincovich turned the place upside down. No luck."

"Figures. But hell, Barney, a zillion people have type A blood," Cid growled, unimpressed.

Barney stood up, trying to work a cramp out of his leg, his long arms hung awkwardly at his sides, his lips barely moving. "That's what I thought . . . until earlier this evening."

"Go on," she prodded, mashing her cigarette.

"Stiff found at Little Capitan tonight was one Carmen Petricelli." The inspector hesitated long enough to see the look of recognition on Cid's face. "I interviewed her when we were investigating Marsha Cox for the Dorset murder. Petricelli tended the Cox family monument and garden at the Cox Funeral Home. Her father worked for the Cox family until Marsha took over the business. She fired him. Carmen Petricelli blamed Marsha for her father's death. She had a huge axe to grind."

"C'mon, Barn, cut to the chase. This is all redundant bullshit." Cid's eyes were troubled.

Barney gave her a brief, wary look and then flipped the pages on his notepad. "Another clean crime scene. Not even any tire tracks. Body was lying in the middle of a small clearing just off the road. As I told you earlier, arms and legs were stretched out in the shape of a cross." The inspector paused. "Sound familiar?"

Cid nodded.

"A single red rose was left just above the head. And get this, one of those arterial tubes morticians use to drain blood was stuck in Petricelli's thigh and a small puddle of blood had formed underneath her. Same M.O. as when Marsha Cox killed the Dorset woman."

Cid drained her glass. Absorbed in thought, she ran her fingers through her gray hair. "Was there anything else?" she asked evenly.

The question seemed to surprise Barney. "Why?"

Adrenaline pumping, Cid sat up. "I want it all, Barn, no holding back."

The inspector's smile was icy; however, he nodded out of respect for Cid's keen investigative mind. "The whole side of Petricelli's head was caved in. Looks like Marsha Cox gave her the boot. There was hardly any blood on her face, so Cox musta worked her over after she was dead."

Now it was Cid's turn to smile. "That's Cox's signature. She abuses her victims after they're dead."

Barney shrugged. "She's slicker than snot. Six weeks ago the chief assigned five detectives, including myself, to track her down. We've staked out her haunts, the funeral home . . . nothing. She gives me the heebie-jeebies."

"She's a serial killer, Barney. She'll give you more than the heebie-jeebies if you don't catch her ass soon."

Thoughtfully, Cid waited until Barney was gone before sliding four singles under her empty highball glass. She picked up the Tums wrapper scraps, placed them in the butt-filled ashtray, and left the bartender to his private thoughts.

Tired springs bounced into action as Cid flopped her bulk behind the steering wheel of the Plymouth and reached to insert her key in the ignition.

Suddenly, a glimmer of light sparkling from the top of the dashboard caught her eye. She blinked twice before leaning closer to inspect a small Vlasic pickle jar that still had part of a label attached to the side. "What the hell . . ." She bit her lower lip. Two small bloody blobs of tissue floated in liquid. She turned on the interior light and studied the contents of the jar more closely. After a few seconds of examination she was sure Melinda Morgan's missing earlobes were now mysteriously in her possession. A shiver ran the length of her back.

Cid locked the car door, quickly turned off the interior lights, and pulled her 9mm from under the seat, cradling the gun between her legs as she checked her rearview mirror. She scanned both sides of the street, paying particular attention to blackened doors and shadowed alleyways. She knew that sociopaths, in their perverse way, liked to terrorize their victims. The more horrific their crimes, the more ghoulish their excitement. She had no doubt somewhere in the darkness, Melinda Morgan's killer was lurking.

The car was filled with uneasy silence as she punched up the number to Tally's car phone. "Damn," she muttered when there was no answer. She left a message and drove with vigilance to police headquarters.

5

Monday, July 6
9:23 P.M.

The area across from the Hall of Justice on Bryant Street and down a narrow alley to the side resembles the strip in Las Vegas. Neon lights blaze in all colors of the rainbow, twenty-four hours a day, advertising the lucrative business of bail bonding. On a busy weekend it's not unusual to see smooth-talking bail bondsmen, or their employees, standing in front of their places of business hawking their services.

As Tally walked along the street she noted the sidewalk was nearly empty of pedestrians; the neighborhood felt safe in the glare of the lights. At the curb she shut her eyes for a minute, waiting for the stoplight to change from red to green. For a split second she permitted herself to think of the paralyzing fear Melinda Morgan must have felt. *She probably knew she was going to die, and in those few moments preceding death she must have felt raw terror. Maybe she tried to reason with her murderer, or maybe she was too frightened to speak.* Tally abruptly opened her eyes and stepped off the curb. She shoved her trembling hands deep into her pants pockets.

As she crossed the street, the aroma of garlic and peppers surrounded her. She smiled as she spotted the small Italian restaurant tucked in between two squat buildings. And the smell immediately transported Tally to her grandmother's kitchen, to the well-worn butcher block, where Grandma often chopped onions and garlic cloves for a tomato sauce. The sauce was a savory delicacy that Tally had never been able to duplicate after her grandmother's death. In that moment she longed to be in that kitchen, enveloped by the warmth of the stove and her grandmother's love.

Coming back to the present with a jolt, Tally stopped in front of a blue neon marquee that flashed the words "Belmondo Bail Bonds." As Tally opened the door and walked into the small, shabby office, Frankie Belmondo came around from behind his dimly lit desk.

"Tally, baby, good to see you." Frankie wore a blue pin-striped shirt paired with a wide floral tie; his pants were held up by bright red suspenders. What little hair he had was slicked back in a dark, glossy cap.

They had met years ago when she was still on patrol. In those days, Frankie lived in uneasy shadows as a police informant, managing somehow to keep a clean record. Eventually he bought the bail business.

Six months before Tally was promoted to inspector she was en route to a loud-and-disorderly complaint, when all hell broke loose. Three Chinese gang members were shot and killed. By the time she and her partner arrived at the scene, most of the party-goers had disappeared. One lonely ten-year-old boy stood in the shadows, too frightened to run. Turned out, he was an innocent bystander who happened by the carnage on his way home from a movie. After Tally determined that the boy saw nothing that would be of use to the police, she quickly shepherded him home, knowing full well if any gang member learned his name, he would be dead. The young boy's father was Frankie Belmondo.

"I need some help," Tally said; her tone revealed her distaste at having to play palsy-walsy with the sleazy bail bondsman.

"Listen, doll," he said with a tight smile, "for you, anything. What are friends for?"

He pointed at a chair adorned with chipped black paint. "Have a seat."

Tally found it easy to imagine Frankie in a stretch limo with an entourage of bodyguards.

He pulled out a shiny gold cigarette case and used a matching gold lighter to fire up a Camel. "What d'ya need?"

"Tell me about morphine."

Frankie sat down in a desk chair covered with burgundy fabric and rested his hands on his ample stomach. "It makes the pain go away." His eyes narrowed. "I post bail bonds; I don't sell drugs."

She nodded. "You're in a tough business, Frankie. I just figured that in dealing with all these low-lifes you might have picked up a little info here and there."

Staring at the ceiling, the bondsman blew small donut-shaped smoke rings into the air. "I hear things."

"Suppose an upper-crust nurse gets hooked and needs a supplier. Where does she go?"

Frankie's grin was sly. "Information like that costs."

Tally returned the smile. "Sure it does, but as you said, what are friends for?"

The bail bondsman tossed his cigarette into a plastic pail filled with sand. "Maybe there's a doctor in town. For a price he writes a prescription. For a bigger hunka change, he supplies."

"Cash on the line?"

"You're talking top drawer, here." His smile showed his yellow teeth. "Credit card . . . check . . . whatever takes care of the obligation."

"How about a line of credit?" she pushed.

He shrugged, thrusting a piece of Juicy Fruit gum into his mouth. "Why not?" he answered between loud smacks.

Tally's voice went cold. "And if she didn't pay?"

Frankie stood up and shoved his hands in his pockets. The conversation was clearly making him uncomfortable. "She might, you know, get roughed up a little."

"That's it?"

"Listen, doll, I'm tellin' ya all I know."

"What if she ran up a sizable bill and wouldn't, or couldn't, pay?"

"Tally, baby, you been on the street, you know the drill. She's dead."

"How, Frankie? How would they kill her?"

He lit another cigarette and inhaled deeply. "Depends on who was sent to do the deed. Business is business."

Tally felt a vile taste in her mouth. "Take a guess."

"Target practice. Ten, maybe fifteen pops."

"How about stabbing?"

Frankie shook his head slowly. "Kid's play. These dudes don't want to soil their hands. Get the picture? There ain't no credit problems in the drug business."

Tally got up and walked to the window. She stared at the vacant street for what seemed a long time. When she turned around her face was expressionless. "I need the doctor's name."

His laugh was low and menacing. "Don't know."

"You have a convenient memory."

"I have a good business I intend to keep." Frankie brushed his meticulously manicured fingers against his shirt.

Tally walked closer. "And if I go down to the Tenderloin and spread the word that you're a snitch, how long will your business thrive?"

His eyes showed his uncertainty. "Sorry, doll, my reputation is solid." A long pause. "Besides, that's blackmail, way below your standards."

Tally chose her words with care. "You're probably right, but then, you taught me that business is business."

Frankie's face looked pale in the glare of blue neon that shone through the front window. "You're a gutsy broad, McGinnis—I admire that. I'll give you what you want . . . and then the slate's clean . . . no more favors . . . no more free info. Got it?" His dark eyes were filled with warning. "The doc's name is Spencer Jewell, M.D."

□□□

The answering service took the emergency message and promised a call back from the doctor in a matter of minutes.

The lights of passing cars flashing against her skin gave Tally a sickly look as she impatiently sat in her car waiting.

Cid's message had left her with an uneasy feeling. *Missing earlobes on the dash of the Plymouth? Who put them there? And why? Was Cid followed? Is she in danger? No, she's at police headquarters, she's safe.* Tally rubbed her forehead and closed her eyes. *Marsha Cox! Did she kill Melinda Morgan? No, it can't be Marsha. It's not her style.*

She had no idea how long she had been thinking, but by the time the telephone finally rang, Tally was so jumpy she nearly dropped the receiver.

The man's voice was abrupt. "Ms. McGinnis? This is Dr. Jewell. I don't recall your name. Have I seen you recently?"

"No, Doctor, we've never met."

"I beg your pardon. I don't do phone consultations for new patients. Are you aware that it's after ten o'clock? Please call my—"

"Not so fast," Tally interrupted before the doctor hung up. "I'm calling for information about Melinda Morgan."

The doctor was silent for a long moment, then he said coolly, "She's not a patient of mine, either. Even if she were, there's the issue of patient confidentiality. I'm sorry, but I must hang up."

"Perhaps if I told you Melinda's problem involved morphine it might stir your memory."

Another long silence. "Who are you?"

"I'm a private investigator working on the Morgan murder. I need information from you."

"As I've already stated, she wasn't my patient."

"That's strange," Tally continued, throwing out the bait. "Sources tell me Melinda saw you shortly before her death."

"Young woman, I don't care what you heard. Melissa or Melinda Morgan was never my patient. Now should you decide to pursue this harassment I'll have to give my dear friend the police commissioner a call."

Tally tried to sound aggrieved. "Dr. Jewell, my call was not intended to harass. I do believe, however, that both public and law enforcement interests will outweigh your petty grievance of harassment once it's known how willingly you use your prescription pad to line your pockets. Call the police commissioner now, because I can assure you, before the night is over, I will call him myself."

Again the doctor was silent for a moment before he responded. "Well . . . I might have seen her once or twice, but I didn't have anything to do with her death." Gracefully, almost too accommodatingly, he added, "Her chart is in order. There were no improprieties."

Tally gave a short laugh. "I'll remember that at your trial."

6

Monday, July 6
10:23 P.M.

An ambulance screamed down Potrero Hill, its light bar flashing red, the driver's face contorted in concentration as he swerved around two cars whose drivers had failed to pull over to the right. Tally watched from the side of the road, nudging the BMW back into traffic after the howling vehicle passed. Two blocks later she pulled into a parking space just across from the entrance to the emergency room at San Francisco General.

Built after the 1906 earthquake, the red brick main hospital building was seven stories tall. Over the years new wings had been added. The entire structure now sprawled over four city blocks and was considered a state-of-the-art facility.

The emergency room was relatively quiet as Tally silently strolled through the glass door entrance.

She observed a doctor in surgical greens standing off to one side quietly speaking with an older man and woman. Then the elevator across the hall opened and a janitor exited, noisily pushing a yellow plastic bucket and mop down the hall. *So much for peace and quiet,* Tally thought.

She stopped at the registration desk and asked for directions to the Pathology Department. Half hidden by a potted palm, a black woman with pearl-rimmed glasses and red hair looked up from her computer. "Building 3, basement," she instructed disinterestedly.

The basement was musty and windowless. The walls had been given a pink face-lift in an apparent effort to brighten things up. Fluorescent lights made the room look as though the paint of choice had been Pepto Bismol.

The pathology lab was down the hall and around the corner, just across from the morgue. The area was eerily cold and damp, and despite the refurbishing efforts, it felt inescapably dim and hollow. Feeble attempts at disguising the stench of death only served to magnify the gross odors. A chill ran the length of Tally's spine as she pushed open the glass door to Pathology.

The bleakly lit room was a study in disorganization. Dirty vials, slides, and pans were stacked in a four-compartment stainless steel sink against one wall. In the corner, two desks, butted up against each other, were overflowing with paperwork. A counter in the center of the room was more organized: several microscopes sat on it in a neat row.

A young man with startlingly white hair sat on a stool hunched over a microscope. He did not hear Tally enter and nearly jumped off his perch when she softly said, "Good evening."

"Ma'am. How can I help ya?" he drawled, leaping to his feet.

"Texas?" Tally guessed. Her grin, white and even, added a certain lightness to her aura of confidence.

"South Carolina, ma'am," he answered proudly, as his hands attempted to iron the wrinkles out of his white lab coat. His hazel eyes were friendly in a face the color of summer peaches. "Town called Goose Creek. You work here at the hospital, ma'am?"

"No. I'm afraid not. Pathology would be my choice if I did. Body pieces and parts and disease have always interested me. And I've got an iron stomach to boot. But I prefer an atmosphere that's a bit more upbeat." She offered her hand. "Tally McGinnis. I'm a private investigator working on Dr. Toliver's case."

The young man's hand went limp in Tally's. "Y'all from the police?"

"No. I work for the doctor's attorney."

He sat down, resting his white Nikes on the rung of the stool. "Johnny Lee, here. And before ya ask, yes, Robert E. is related to me. Just no one in the family can figure out if he's a fifth or sixth cousin once removed. I don't know beans about the Civil War and, to be perfectly honest, I don't know a helluva lot about Robert E. either. The white hair runs in the family. Great-granddaddy musta had a flawed gene, cuz his hair was as white as grits 'fore he turned twenty-five. The rest of us Lees have followed suit. Medicine's my game, and as far as I'm concerned, all them Civil War heroes were just a bunch of good ol' boys. Now you take Dr. Toliver . . . she's a real hero."

Tally smiled in a not-so-subtle way, unsure whether to laugh or applaud. "You're a doctor?"

"No ma'am. Lab tech. Becky—that is, Dr. Toliver—paid my way through school. She and Melinda let me live with them till I got on my feet. Moved into my own apartment 'bout a year and a half ago. That's what I mean 'bout bein' a hero. She's got a heart the size of this here state."

"So you're both a friend and a coworker?"

"Yes, ma'am. Becky and Melinda were 'bout the two best people on this earth." His tone became dismissive. "I know what the Bible says 'bout people like that, you know, livin' together and all. Hell, my

mama'd have a hissy fit if she knew 'bout them. But it
plum don't matter to me none."

A flush crept up Tally's neck. "How did they get
along?" she asked, sensing that Johnny Lee was not the
liberal he pretended to be.

"You sure I'm supposed to be talkin' to you like
this?"

"Yes," Tally answered truthfully.

"I lived there near two years, never heard them
have a cross word. They were like best friends. I mean
they never showed affection in front of me, but there
sure were a lot of nights the bedroom door was closed,"
he said vehemently.

"How long have you worked at San Francisco
General?"

"Near five years now," he answered proudly.
"Worked part-time all the while I was goin' to school.
Becky hired me full-time soon as I got my tech license."

Tally walked over to a microscope, rested one
hand on the base, and asked curiously, "Have you
always worked the same hours as the doctor?"

"Since I been full-time. We work a four-day,
forty-hour week. Tuesday through Friday. Four P.M. tuh
two A.M. I like the hours; it gives me three days off a
week. Since Becky's been gone, I been workin'
Mondays, too. Sure hope she gets back soon."

"So you were working the Friday Melinda was
murdered?"

Johnny Lee tried to keep his face impassive, but
his apprehension showed. "Yes."

Tally's tone was gentle. "Was Dr. Toliver in the
habit of leaving the lab for long periods of time?"

Johnny's eyes shut. "Police were here the day
after it happened." He opened his eyes and looked
across the room as if someone were standing there.
"You know, after Melinda died, I answered their

questions best I could. I don't wanta hurt Becky none, so what you're askin', you *sure* this is gonna help her?"

Tally stepped forward. Even with the lab technician sitting on the high stool, her five-foot-nine-inch frame was several inches taller than the seated young man. She silently nodded.

Johnny's hazel eyes fixed on Tally's. "She hardly ever left. I mean, she'd go to the rest room and sometimes if I was out on a break she'd run upstairs to surgery to pick up a stat biopsy or somethin'. Otherwise she was here. Even ate at her desk."

Tally watched him uneasily. He sounded rehearsed, a bit too accommodating. "That Friday night, were you here when she left?"

"Yes, ma'am." Johnny kept his voice steady. "Left at eight forty-five. I just got back from my dinner break. Didn't see her again until near eleven o'clock."

"Did she seem upset when she returned?"

Johnny leaned back, clasping his hands at the back of his head. "I could tell she'd been crying. Eyes were puffy. Red. She's got hair the color of honey, always looks just so. Not that night. It was flyin' all over the place. Looked like she'd stood beside a herd of horses on the run."

His dark eyes narrowed until they looked almost reptilian. "You sure this ain't gonna hurt her none?" His hands played nervously with the knobs on the microscope.

"What else did you notice about her?"

A slight hesitation was apparent in his voice. "Blood on her lab coat and a dribble or two on her scrubs. Here." He rubbed his hand down his right arm. "And here." His hand continued across his chest.

"Go on."

"She sat at her desk for a while. I knew she didn't wanta talk. Wouldn't even look at me. 'Bout fifteen minutes later she up and walked over to the

Contaminated box." Johnny pointed at a large red container sitting in the corner. "We put our gloves and paper aprons in there for burning. Anyways, she pulled off her lab coat, stuffed it in, and got a clean one from the closet. 'Bout 11:30 she told me to clean up the sink. It's supposed to get done every night. Without her here, nothin' gets done."

"Did you tell the police about the lab coat?"

Johnny fidgeted with a glass slide sitting on the microscope, then hopped off the stool. "No. Don't intend to neither." At the sink he pulled on a pair of thick rubber gloves and began filling an autoclave with dirty scalpels.

Tally watched him. "There's more . . . what is it?"

He lowered his eyes, his hands still clutching the autoclave door. The silence lengthened. A wall had gone up. Tally wasn't sure whether Johnny's pose was part of a well-rehearsed drama or whether he truly was afraid he'd revealed too much already.

"There ain't no more. Now just leave me be. I got work to do."

"Johnny," Tally pleaded.

Silence.

"Did anyone else see the bloody lab coat?"

He shook his head.

Tally felt a rush of anger. "How about time? Can someone vouch for you between eight forty-five and eleven?"

"Ma'am, my mama didn't raise no fool. And I ain't 'bout to be the one sitting in jail." With new defiance, he shifted his shoulders back and stood razor straight. "If you'll be needin' somethin' else, you just talk to Becky. Otherwise, I don't know nothin'. Now if you'll excuse me, like I said, I got work to do." His look was dismissive.

"Just one more thing, Johnny: what did you think of Melinda? Was she a good nurse?"

All defensiveness vanished. "Florence Nightingale. Finest woman I ever met. Best nurse at this here hospital. Ask anyone." His voice held pleasure, his look bliss.

Johnny's behavior bothered Tally. As she stood waiting for the elevator she thought about his attitude. She hadn't been able to see inside of him, to guess what he was really feeling. He had told her what he wanted her to hear, nothing more. She was struck by Johnny's innocent posture and the ease with which he'd incriminated Rebecca Toliver. And she was shaken by the fact that he had taken control of the interrogation. She felt manipulated.

Had Tally not been acutely aware of her surroundings she probably would have missed what happened next: she heard what seemed to be the sound of clothes brushing against the wall. Tally turned quickly and was sure she saw a figure dart around the corner of the hallway at the same instant the elevator door opened. Heart pounding, she hastily stepped inside the elevator and frantically stabbed at the Door Close button.

As the elevator rose, Tally decided that very probably Johnny Lee had been the figure lurking in the shadows, but that thought did nothing to calm her trembling hands.

"PEDIATRICS" was printed in bold letters on a glass partition at the third-floor nursing station. Tally presented herself to a tall male with a broad face and tiny piercing brown eyes.

"I'd like to speak with the director of nursing."

Dressed in white, he carefully returned a metal chart to the file before looking up. "Perhaps I can help.

I'm the charge nurse. The director of nursing works day shift." A red-and-white name tag pinned to his lab coat had both his name, Karl Klump, and his title.

Tally introduced herself and explained why she was there. They shook hands and then the nurse stepped back, as if to have a better look.

"Is it hard to stay awake working the night shift?" Tally asked, wondering how much, if anything, he knew about what happened to Melinda Morgan.

"Naw, we get used to it." He tilted his head, considering her. "How can I help?'

"To start, was Melinda Morgan a good nurse?"

Karl smiled. "You need Human Resources, the hospital personnel office. I'm not allowed to give out information like that."

Tally studied him. "Did you know Melinda well?"

"Oh, yes," he said, a veil of grief evident in his voice. "Very well. I was a pallbearer at her funeral. Loved her like a sister. She transferred up to Pediatrics because of me. I mean she loved the kids, but we enjoyed working together, too."

Slowly, Tally's eyes locked on his. She sensed he not only wanted to talk, he needed to grieve. This time she was gentler when she pressed. "Was everything okay on the job?"

He bowed his head and nodded. "Yes. She was a good nurse. But, listen, I could lose my job talking to you like this."

Respectfully, she said, "I understand what a difficult position I'm putting you in, but for Melinda's sake, and Dr. Toliver's, as well, tell me what you know."

Karl Klump shrugged.

She watched his face. "Okay, let's try this from another angle. You told me she performed her job well. I will assume there were no problems here at the hospital." She studied him, waiting for him to protest her assumption. When he did not, she continued. "I just met with Johnny Lee, Dr. Toliver's lab tech. Any problems there?"

Karl Klump frowned. "The only good thing about Melinda's death is that little twerp isn't hanging around here anymore." He paused, leaning forward, checking the hallway. "Every night, every break, he was here. He'd hang on every word she said. Touch her hand. Touch her back. Even pinch her cheek. Brought her little presents. It got to the point, when she was home alone she bolted her doors and stayed inside."

"She must have protested."

"Oh, she did." Karl abruptly stood straight. "At first she tried to laugh him off. Then, despite the fact she didn't want to hurt him, she told him he couldn't come up to Peds anymore. He's a persistent, selfish bastard. He ignored her request and still came here every night. Trailed after her like a sick puppy. Finally, after I talked with her, she sat him down, right here, as a matter of fact." He pointed to a chrome stool on wheels. "She told him she was writing him up and sending the report to personnel, and if he came up to the Peds floor again she'd call security."

Tally gathered herself. "When did this happen?"

"Night before she was murdered." The fierceness in Karl's eyes intensified.

Tally felt her stomach knot. "Melinda worked at the hospital for years—why didn't she report him sooner?"

"She worked in another building; Johnny Lee never bothered her over there. But Johnny has a history here at the hospital. He stalked another nurse about a year ago. She got fed up and quit. Went to work at a nursing home."

Tally grimaced. "Did the nurse report Johnny to the personnel office or police?"

The edge to Karl's voice was submerged in grief. "No. And ironically," he said, his eyes now red rimmed, "neither did Melinda. She threw the report in the garbage. She just couldn't bring herself to hurt Johnny Lee; she felt sorry for him."

Tally's face was grim now. "Did you tell the police about Johnny?"

"They never questioned me—only the nursing director."

"Why didn't you come forward?"

"Hospital doesn't like this type of publicity. It was bad enough Dr. Toliver was arrested. Management didn't tell us not to cooperate, but they implied as much. I learned a long time ago not to buck authority. People can get fired for strange reasons. I'm a gay male nurse. There's not supposed to be discrimination on the job, but we all know it's here. I'd do anything for Melinda, but where she is now—well, losing my job isn't going to help her. I've taken the risk of talking to you. If you want the police to know about Johnny Lee, you tell them."

Tally extended her hand. "Thank you," she said warmly.

As an afterthought she asked, "How were Dr. Toliver and Melinda as a couple? Happy?"

Quietly Karl folded his hands in front of him. "They loved each other and seemed happy." He raised his head. "But a couple of weeks before Melinda died she came to work with a bruise on her face. She said she bumped her cheek on the car door, but I'm a nurse— you can't fool me easily. It looked like a handprint to me. You know, like someone slapped her hard. Since Dr. Toliver was arrested I've wondered if Melinda was protecting her, just like she was protecting Johnny Lee."

It was well past midnight when she cautiously walked across the hospital parking lot. As she reviewed Karl Klump's words, a feeling of sadness overcame her. With every murder case she had ever worked on, there came a time when she imagined what the murder victim experienced, emotionally and physically, just before they took their last breath. Now, as she approached her BMW with keys in hand, her despair was overwhelming. Melinda Morgan had died with little resolution in her life. She was addicted to drugs, stalked by a sick young man, and in all probability, was involved in a troubled relationship. With three swift blows from a scalpel, a vicious murderer had halted any hope Melinda Morgan might have had of righting the wrongs in her life.

As she slipped her key into the lock, Tally noticed the fog had left a light dew on her car. Suddenly, from out of nowhere, an arm wrapped around her neck in a viselike grip, a powerful forearm crushing her throat. Furiously, she struggled. Then, momentarily relaxing, she waited for her attacker's grip to ease. When it did, Tally slammed her elbow into her assailant's gut, then stomped down hard on the booted foot.

Suddenly, she was flung to the ground, and landed with a thud. There was no time to reach for the .38 she carried in the small of her back.

Dazed, she tasted blood and heard fast, labored breathing. Without warning, something sharp tore at her cheek. She screamed. The attacker grabbed her hair and viciously slammed her face into the pavement. The last thing Tally remembered was the parking lot lights dimming.

7

Tuesday, July 7
7:54 A.M.

The night had turned out a disaster. Sleep had not come for Tally. Strangers in the shadows ambushed her mind and plagued her dreams. Bloody scalpels and faceless corpses greeted every toss and turn. Her head pounded, and her cheek ached and still stung from the antiseptic the doctor had applied in the emergency room.

Finally, at four forty-five, only two hours after she had arrived at the office, Tally had rolled off the office couch and into the shower. The little greasy spoon at the marina provided a cholesterol-fortified breakfast of eggs, sausage, and hash browns. But it did not dispel the anxious knot in her stomach, or the memory of the previous night's attack.

After two cups of coffee, Tally felt more able to tackle the day, and returned to the office. As she walked into the Phoenix Detective Agency, the sight of Katie made her smile. In her late twenties, Katie O'Neil was a concentrated champagne bubble—gay, zestful, her face cheerful, smooth, and fringed with shoulder-length curly brown hair. She kept herself in shape by running at least five miles daily. Her blue eyes were ever so grand, filled with Irish mischief and deep love for Tally McGinnis.

Katie froze at the sight of Tally and dropped the papers in her hand. "My God," she gasped, quickly rounding her desk. "What happened?"

Tally was not quite ready to talk. She opened her arms and Katie ran forward to meet her. For a time, they simply held each other.

Katie leaned back, her eyes on Tally's. "Who did this to you?"

"I'm not sure. It happened in the hospital parking lot. Police wrote it up as a mugging, but nothing was taken. I was knocked out, but no concussion thankfully. My cheek—" Tally reached up and gingerly touched the bloody scratches— "was intentionally scraped. The doctor removed a couple of pieces of gravel. Before I left the hospital the police found a battered red rose under my car."

Katie's body tensed and her eyes held fear. "Last evening, before I went home, Cid told me about this new murder case. Are you, too, believing this is the work of Marsha Cox?"

Tally drew her close again. "I don't know," she answered in a flat voice. "Things just don't add up. And having my head pounded into the pavement certainly isn't making the picture any clearer."

"Will it never stop?"

"Crime?" Tally asked.

Katie nodded.

"Not so long as we humans covet what others have. Money and love are the two main ingredients for crime. Unless of course the demon is, as Cid is fond of saying, a sicko like Marsha Cox. With a serial killer like her, who knows what the motivator might be."

Katie was quiet for a moment. "And what about you, Tally McGinnis? Where do you stand on love? You've not come to our bed for five nights now; surely you must be weary of the couch." She pulled away, walking across the room and turning her back to Tally.

Tally's voice was gentle. "I saw no reason to wake you last night. It was late and I wasn't hurt badly, so I slept here, at the office, love."

Katie turned to her. "And your fear? Could I not have comforted you?" The room was filled with silence. "Da used to say, 'It's better to live in the forest with a carpet of leaves for a bed and wee critters for companions, than to choose a cold castle built on a hill of silence and loneliness.' We must come to some sort of understanding, or the grand love we share will surely be lost."

Ambivalence pulled at Tally's heart as she stared deeply into Katie's blue eyes. Awkwardly she said, "I've lived alone for some time. I'm used to coming and going as I please. I truly am not trying to be selfish; I'm just set in my ways and need a little time to adjust."

Katie sat down at her desk and picked up the packet of papers she had dropped earlier. "Is it really about adjustment, Tally McGinnis, or are you afraid of commitment?"

Tally's expression did not change, but her heart was banging in her chest. The fear of losing Katie was so overwhelming she nearly cried out. She stepped around the desk and rested her hands on Katie's shoulders. The raw feeling in her voice was powerful when she finally spoke.

"I'm sorry. Time? Commitment? I'm not sure, Katie, but I know I love you."

Katie stopped herself from turning around. "Open your heart just a wee bit more, Tally, and let me all the way in. If the love is there, the commitment will come." Her eyes had filled with tears, but her voice was steady. "And this," she said, waving the papers in her hand, "will surely help the process along."

The ends of Tally's strawberry bangs dipped down across her right eye and brushed Katie's cheek as

she leaned forward to more closely view the cruise ship
tickets and boarding instructions in Katie's hand.

"We leave in a week," Katie announced, feigning
happiness. "You're sure this new case won't interfere
with the trip?"

Tally lightly touched her lips to Katie's cheek,
then gracefully reached for a cup and poured herself a
fresh Cafe Vienna. She sipped the soothing coffee as she
considered Katie's question. "I'm sure," she finally
answered, not sounding the least bit convincing.

Tally opened the sapphire-colored drapes and
stood looking out the vast expanse of glass, letting the
morning sun caress her weary body. Her green eyes,
accented with just a hint of emerald eye shadow,
scanned the office workers and professionals hurrying
by on the sidewalk below. She thought of her attacker
from the night before. She knew someone had been
watching her and guessed that the voyeur was out
there, silently stalking. She wished herself invisible.

Turning from the window abruptly, she said,
"Katie, please start a new file labeled 'Rebecca Toliver'
and give Rita Cruz's office a call. The fee schedule
should be the same as the last case we handled for her:
two hundred an hour plus expenses. Make sure she
understands that both Cid and I charge that hourly rate,
so a good part of the time she'll be paying $400 an hour.
Also, I want a $10,000 retainer."

Katie whistled. "'Tis a nice piece of change." Her
Irish brogue was thick.

Tally set her coffee cup on the desk and walked
across the reception area. When she turned back, she
looked at Katie, without really seeing her. "Also, please
call Goose Creek, a town in South Carolina. See if you
can find out anything about a fellow named Johnny
Lee: where he went to school, who his friends were, if
he's ever been in any trouble." Tally fell silent. The
mention of his name was disturbing. Brushing a thread

from her denim shirt she added, "I don't want him to know we're checking, so be discreet."

Without warning, Cid barged through the door. Her hair was standing on end and dark circles lay beneath her eyes. Inspector Barney Hampton was close on her heels. She brushed past both women without acknowledgment.

"Good to see you, too," Katie called after Cid. "A little too much scotch last night?"

"No!"

"It's always a pleasure, Cidney," Katie teased. She swiveled her desk chair around to face Tally. "Top of the morning and good luck."

Tally looked at the clock as if it were a frame of reference. She was disturbed by the appearance of Barney Hampton. "When you call Rita's office, leave word that I need to speak with her." With that, she walked down the hall.

Tally flopped wearily into a red upholstered chair that sat directly across from Cid's desk. The chair had been another of Victoria McGinnis's estate sale finds. It was a beautiful piece of furniture, but better suited for a Victorian museum. Both Tally and Cid found the chair's high, rigid back and skimpy padding to be very uncomfortable.

Other than a picture of Sadie on her desk, Cid's office was bare of any personal effects. A black leather couch that had been in the conference room sat in the middle of the office looking like a misplaced modifier. The walls were bare except for a print of Van Gogh's *Starry Night* that Tally had brought from home.

Barney Hampton sat on one end of the couch sipping coffee from a McDonald's styrofoam cup. Cid stood behind him, her anger clearly apparent.

"Face looks good, Tal." Cid's words were dipped in sarcasm. "Thanks to Barney here, I was clued in about your attack. After all, other than being your business partner, why call me and let me know you were mugged?"

Tally's eyes searched Cid's as she draped her legs over the arm of the chair and allowed her brown Birkenstocks to fall to the floor. "This must be dump on Tally Day." Wearily, she said, "I didn't call you, and I didn't wake up Katie, because I thought the two of you might like your rest. Next time I stub my toe I'll be sure to give you a call."

"Stub your toe! For Christ's sake, Tal, someone attacked you. Could have killed you."

"That's enough!" Barney Hampton stood up and tossed his empty coffee cup in the wastebasket. "You two work out your partnership disagreements on your own time. What happened last night, McGinnis?"

There was no hiding her irritation. "I'm sure you were privy to the police report or the two of you wouldn't have come in this morning with both barrels loaded."

His eyes got hard. "Don't mess with me, McGinnis; I'm not above charging you with obstruction of justice."

Tally slammed her feet on the floor. Her face flared red. She wasn't backing down. "You just do that, Inspector Hampton, and you'll look like the dumb flatfoot you are. When we last met you had me under suspicion for Cathy Dorset's murder. That turned out to be a fine waste of taxpayer dollars. An inept bungle that allowed Marsha Cox her freedom. Now you're at it again. In case you had trouble reading the report from last night, *I'm* the innocent party, the *victim* who got mugged. What's with you?"

"Just walking across the hospital parking lot, were you?" he asked, sarcastically.

"Yes." Tally slipped her shoes back on and stood. "I was jumped from behind. I didn't see who it was."

"And nothing was missing?"

"No."

"Why did he or she jump you then?"

Tally resisted the opportunity for another attack on the inspector and sat back down. "I suspect it was some sort of warning."

Cid lit a cigarette and moved around to the couch.

"Meaning what?" Barney Hampton asked, clearly interested.

Moments passed. "I'm not sure." Tally touched her cheek. "Patrol found a red rose next to my car."

Barney looked at Cid and then back at Tally. His eyes were keen. "Anything else?"

"No."

"Your attacker didn't say anything?"

"No."

"Male or female?"

"I'm not sure. Very strong."

"Maybe you noticed an odor? You know, deodorant, garlic breath, hair oil?"

She hesitated. "There was something." She rubbed her forehead. "I just can't put my finger on it. Can't remember. Everything happened so damn fast."

It was a moment before Barney stopped scrutinizing Tally. "Were you packing a piece?"

"Yes," Tally answered. "My .38."

"Why didn't you use it?"

Tally shook her head. "I can't believe I'm hearing this. *I was jumped from the rear.*"

Hampton walked closer and gave Tally a mock once over. "Strange your gun and wallet weren't taken."

"You should be fired for incompetence," Tally sneered.

Barney Hampton pointed his finger at Tally. "Consider yourself lucky, McGinnis—your ass could be

in jail. Remember, it was you alone who reported
Marsha Cox had confessed to killing Cathy Dorset. No
police officer ever heard that confession, and as far as
I'm concerned, the case is wide open . . . and you're still
as good a suspect as any.

"As to your claim that someone jumped you, I
find the whole incident suspicious, particularly the part
about a red rose."

Anger filled the room. "Be vigilant, McGinnis—"
Inspector Hampton licked his lips and again pointed
his finger—"because I'm watching every move you
make."

Turning away, Barney popped two Tums in his
mouth. "Call me later," he said to Cid, and left without
saying good-bye.

Cid walked to her desk. "No love lost between
the two of you."

"Keep him out of this office," Tally said, the
fierceness in her eyes undiminished.

"Haven't got control of that, Tal. Besides, he's
just posturing, yanking your chain. Barney likes being
in the driver's seat. You know, the authority figure. He
knows when you're angry he's in total control . . . so he
eggs you on by constantly pegging you as a suspect.
Ignore his bullshit and he'll leave you alone. Besides, he
thinks Marsha Cox and Rebecca Toliver killed Melinda
Morgan." She picked up a yellow legal pad. "You
okay?"

"You mean aside from having to deal with that
idiot?" Tally half shrugged. "My cheek is killing me. My
head doesn't hurt at all." She smiled faintly. "But then,
that doesn't surprise you, does it?"

Cid returned the smile. "No, I'd be more
concerned about the probable crack in the pavement.
Hard heads make a fierce weapon."

They both laughed.

Cid sat down in her judge's chair. "You've had a busy night. Tell me what you learned."

Tally quickly filled her in about Johnny Lee and Karl Klump.

"Do you think Johnny Lee jumped you in the parking lot?" Cid asked.

Tally considered this for a moment. "I don't think so. Johnny Lee is short. Maybe five-five or five-six. I think my attacker was taller. And Johnny would have no reason to leave a rose. There's one other thing. Barney asked if I'd noticed an odor. I'm not totally sure, but I think I might have smelled peppermint, like maybe my attacker was chewing gum. I'm just not completely sure. It's still jumbled in my head. Still can't believe someone got the drop on me." Her voice took on a slight edge. "Being the benefactor of two earlobes doesn't sound like your evening was any less eventful than mine. Who do you think left them for you?"

Cid's tone was dry. "No doubt it was Marsha Cox. She likes games. The more macabre the better."

Tally jumped to her feet and began pacing. "It makes no sense, Cid. Earlobes! That's small-fry to Marsha Cox. If she wanted to shock you, by God, she'd do it right. She'd lop off someone's head and leave the bloody remains dripping on your dash. A pickle jar with a couple of earlobes doesn't fit her M.O. She's a vicious, sadistic killer who loves the glory of her acts."

Cid leaned back in her chair, her heavily starched white shirt scratching against the leather. "Sorry, Tal, there's just too much evidence pointing directly at Marsha Cox. For example: the stiff found at Little Capitan Park last night was one Carmen Petricelli." She studied Tally for a moment. "The same Carmen Petricelli who helped you on the Dorset case, the one who gave you incriminating information about Marsha Cox."

Tally collapsed in her chair, her eyes fixed on Cid. "Oh God," she moaned. She thought of the refined, elegant woman who had been so helpful, so eager to see Marsha brought to justice. "How?" She managed to whisper, her voice heavy with sadness.

"You know her modus operandi." Cid's eyes gave off an icy glare. "An arterial tube in the femoral artery. She was bled to death and then had the crap kicked out . . ."

Tally felt an awful emptiness and more than a little guilt. "What else? Was she only bled to death and kicked?"

Cid roughly lit a cigarette. "Jesus, Tal. Woman's dead. Bled to death. Body mutilated. What more do you want?"

Tally was persistent. "Was she mutilated or kicked? Were her earlobes removed?"

"Damn, I don't know. Didn't see the body. Barney said kicked. I don't understand where you're going with this."

"If this murder is Marsha Cox's work," Tally said slowly, "we should be seeing more conspicuous signs of violence. Remember, Cox is a woman who has begun to unravel. Her compulsion should be taking over. We should see some mistakes."

"Unravel? Shit, she's getting bolder." Cid stood and began pacing back and forth across the beige carpet.

Again Tally thought of Carmen, picturing her fine white hair and vibrant blue eyes. *Something's not right.*

"Sorry to interrupt," Katie said, lightly tapping on the doorframe. "Rita Cruz is on line one." She turned to face Tally. "She's off to court, only has a moment."

Tally took the call in her office. A panoramic view of the city surrounded her. Unlike Cid's impersonal office decor, Tally's walls were covered with San Francisco 49ers memorabilia, her college degree, and her private detective license. As she greeted Rita her voice was calm, professional, and to the point. "It's time Cid and I met your client."

The busy attorney was silent as she quickly scanned her planner. "I can't meet with you," she said in a matter-of-fact voice, "but I will make arrangements for you to see her in the interview room at Justice. When?" Her tone was clipped.

"This morning."

Rita exhaled. "I'll do my best. My secretary will get back to you shortly. And, Tal," she added smoothly, "my appointment with District Attorney John Plummer is at one o'clock tomorrow. I expect some action. Four hundred dollars an hour should buy some answers." The line went dead.

8

Tuesday, July 7
11:02 A.M.

The upper floors at the Hall of Justice were a maze of tiny, cramped offices, worn green tile, and patched white walls. The county jail, on the sixth and seventh floors, served as a human storage tank. The pungent smell of urine seemed to cling to the skin; the constant bedlam of the incarcerated shouting at each other made visitors and inmates alike feel crazed and helpless. Sickly fluorescent lights added to the dreariness.

Dr. Rebecca Toliver was housed on the sixth floor. Cid and Tally waited for her in the one interview room set aside for women.

The room had once been a closet and was barely wide enough to accommodate a table and two chairs. The walls were painted the color of banana pudding; dirty fingerprints left a trail around the light switch. A shatterproof window overlooking the corridor stretched the length of the room. A guard kept a constant vigil, his eyes scanning the room for any sign of trouble. To protect prisoner rights, no recording or listening devices were allowed.

Cid sat at the table, a lighted cigarette dangling from her mouth, her fingers absently drumming on the Formica tabletop. Tally stood with her back against the wall, notepad and pencil in hand. She found it difficult not to think about what her client might have done.

When Dr. Toliver was led into the room, both Cid and Tally were surprised to see that she walked with a limp and leaned heavily on the guard's arm for support. She wore a prison-issued orange jumpsuit and her honey-colored hair rested lightly on her shoulders. Rebecca Toliver was a plain-looking woman with a rather large nose, and lips that rested naturally in a gentle smile. She wore glasses with blue wire rims.

The women quickly introduced themselves. The door was closed. A third chair the guard had brought into the room barely fit between the end of the table and the wall. Tally squeezed into the chair and took the lead. "I wish we had the luxury of getting to know one another, but I'm sure you're aware that your attorney, Rita Cruz, meets with the D.A. tomorrow and we have nothing at this point that would begin to suggest a reason for him to reduce charges or consider a bond for you." Tally seemed to be forming her words carefully so as not to offend this plain, yet appealing, woman. "In fact, Doctor, so far the evidence seems to favor the prosecution."

Rebecca Toliver folded her slender hands in front of her as she appraised Tally and Cid. "Is there a predetermined fee you and your agency expect to earn before you turn evidence in my favor over to my attorney? If that's the case, I'd prefer paying you the money up front to speed up the process." Her eyes narrowed.

Her comment changed the atmosphere abruptly.

Cid made a production out of dropping her cigarette to the cement floor and smothering it under her black loafer. "We don't withhold evidence to make more money." Her jaw muscles flexed. "What Tally was trying to tell you is that everywhere we turn, you look guilty as hell."

Tally leaned back against the wall, her chair scraping a groove in the plaster. "If you would like to remove us from your case we'll leave now," she said patiently. "But frankly, Doctor, you need all the help you can get."

"I never said that I wished to remove you from my case. I merely suggested the possibility that you or someone with lesser ethics might take advantage of the opportunity for financial gain before producing information that would help me."

"Jesus," Cid breathed, in her best I-can't-believe-what-I'm-hearing voice. "Let's just get on with this."

"Please," the doctor responded coolly.

Looking down at her notepad Tally asked, "Why did you fire your first two lawyers?"

The doctor waited to answer as if recalling a painful memory. "When I was first brought here for booking the only lawyer I knew was Charles Cook. He'd handled a malpractice suit for a friend of mine. He came right down to the Hall of Justice, but it was clear from the moment he arrived that criminal law was not his specialty. I didn't really fire him, just switched to an attorney who was better qualified to handle my predicament."

Cid watched and listened, her eyes cold and unfriendly.

"And your second attorney?"

"H. Q. Bryant." The doctor's leg seemed to be bothering her. She carefully maneuvered it farther under the table using both her hands. "I fired him this week. He was going nowhere with my case. I've been incarcerated for more than a month and the best he could offer was a plea bargain."

The doctor leaned forward, her brown eyes intense and intelligent. "Melinda is dead. She was my light. My life. He wanted me to tell the world I had killed her . . ." Her voice trailed off as she lowered her head.

Cid reached in the pocket of the same navy Dockers she had worn the day before and pulled out her Virginia Slims and lighter.

"Please," Rebecca said, meeting Cid's intense glare, "I have asthma."

Cid groaned, but left the pack of cigarettes lying on the table. "Where were you the night Melinda was murdered?"

"At work. San Francisco General."

"Right," Cid snapped sarcastically. "And your car drove itself to your house."

"Cid—" Tally nodded toward the door— "go have a smoke." It was the good cop, bad cop routine, only this time it hadn't been planned.

"It's okay," Rebecca exhaled. She looked vulnerable and tired. "You didn't ask me how my car got to our house; you asked where I was when Melinda was murdered. I repeat, I was at work."

Removing her glasses, the doctor rubbed her eyes. "My job doesn't warrant high visibility."

"That's true." Tally spoke calmly. "But you weren't in your lab, either."

"You've spoken with Johnny, I trust?"

Tally nodded.

The doctor put her glasses back on, leaned back in her chair, and rested her head against the wall. "You must understand that my work ethic is very strong. I run my department with strict adherence to the rules. Johnny Lee is a superb lab technician and a good man, I might add, but he is not a highly motivated worker. I hold him accountable for his work. He responds to authority by being passively aggressive."

"Which means what?" Cid asked.

"He's not always truthful."

The last observation seemed carefully planted, Tally thought. "I didn't get that impression of Johnny at all. In fact he spoke highly of both you and Melinda."

"I never said Johnny didn't care about me; I merely wanted to make you aware that he doesn't always report the facts accurately."

"So you're calling him a liar?" Cid persisted.

The doctor pushed forward in her chair, eyes wide. "No. I'm saying that if Johnny were disciplined on the job, which he was on the day in question, he might not report the day's events accurately. It would be his passive way of getting even."

"So where were you?" Cid asked, slowly enunciating each word.

The doctor's brown eyes flashed. "I left my work station at eight forty-five and I returned at five minutes after eleven. There's a storage room next to the lab, and a year ago I had a small metal desk and chair put in it for my use. Sometimes I like the solitude."

Tally and Cid looked at each other, but said nothing.

"What do you remember about the night Melinda was murdered?" Tally asked.

It was a question the doctor had been dreading. "I try not to remember."

"Why?"

"Because it was traumatic." For a brief moment the doctor was silent. Her eyes held pain. "If I dwell on that night, it forces me to think about Melinda. To realize she's gone." She shut her eyes, trying to chase away the memory.

"After your shift was over, what time did you leave the hospital?"

"About five after two."

"You went straight home?" Tally pushed.

"Yes. I could see the red and blue lights flashing as I came down the street. I ran up the walkway to the house, but the police wouldn't let me past the living room. At some point—I don't remember exactly when—I was told Melinda was dead. Shortly after that, a plainclothes policeman asked if he could search my car. I later learned that was Inspector Hampton. You must understand—" the doctor's voice quivered— "I was so upset . . . I had nothing to hide; I gave him my keys." Tears slipped from the corners of her eyes.

Tally fished a tissue from the pocket of her white cotton pants and handed it to the doctor. "Then what?"

"They were laughing." Tears continued to roll down her cheeks, but the doctor's voice and eyes conveyed outrage. "In our dining room, two, three police officers and a news reporter from KRON." Rebecca Toliver looked at Cid and then at Tally, her hands spread in a helpless gesture. "They were talking and laughing about the size of Melinda's breasts. Mel was dead for God's sake. There was no respect, no dignity."

Cid lowered her eyes and rubbed her forehead. She had seen and heard the jokes so many times before.

"I'm sorry," Tally said softly. She knew the pain and anguish on the doctor's face were real.

"What about Marsha Cox?" Cid asked in her driest voice. "When did you first meet her?"

The doctor dabbed at her eyes; her expression was puzzled. "Who?"

"Marsha Cox. Cox Funeral Home on Nob Hill."

Rebecca Toliver shook her head slowly, the look of puzzlement still on her face. "My job requires me to deal with mortuaries, so of course I've heard of Cox Funeral Home and I may have met Marsha Cox a time or two."

"A time or two?" Cid questioned. "Sure you're not lovers?"

"Don't be absurd. I said I *may* have met her a time or two."

Cid dismissed the question with a wave of her hand. "Your leg. You were limping when you came in. Is that a recent . . .?"

"No, I had cancer when I was a child. My leg was amputated just below the knee. I wear a prosthesis. I'm not as agile as some—that's why I normally use a cane."

"I see." Cid tilted her head to one side and asked, "Is that why the wicker basket in your hallway was knocked over the night Melinda was murdered?"

The doctor's eyes went cold. "Just who are you working for Ms. Cameron—me or the police?"

It was time, Cid knew, to shift the focus. "Tell us a little more about Johnny Lee."

"Yes, Doctor," Tally added, "I find him interesting."

Rebecca Toliver stared coldly at Cid and then shifted her attention to Tally. "Please feel free to call me Becky." She paused, as if gathering her thoughts. "Johnny Lee came to San Francisco General about five years ago. I'm sure you know he's from South Carolina. He was eighteen when I first met him. His home life had not been good . . . his father was an alcoholic and abuse was rampant in the household. Mel and I opened our home to Johnny. He was a pleasure to have around." She laughed at the memory. "He brought out Mel's motherly instincts. She baked cookies, ironed his clothes, and generally spoiled him rotten. When he finished school we gave him the first month's rent for his own apartment and a new bedroom set as a gift. He was a good companion and houseguest. No dark shadows in his past that I'm aware of. Melinda knew Johnny more intimately then I do. I'm his boss; I've had to maintain a certain professional relationship."

"Did he favor you over Melinda or vice versa?" Tally coached patiently.

Rebecca blinked. "Neither. As I indicated earlier, Johnny plays games, but nothing that Mel and I couldn't handle."

"And you're sure he wasn't in love with Melinda?"

The doctor seemed surprised by the question. "Of course not; he knew Melinda was my partner and respected that fact." A flicker of doubt briefly crossed the doctor's face.

"Was she having an affair with anyone?"

Rebecca froze, feeling the sting of the question. "No!"

There was a fierceness about Tally as she met the doctor's eyes. "What about drugs. Did Johnny know Melinda was addicted to morphine?"

The doctor's resolve collapsed. Her shoulders sagged and she looked down at her hands. Her fingers were white from squeezing them tightly together. "He did not know." She formed her words slowly. "No one knew."

"Were you trying to protect her?" Cid asked, her tone suddenly patient, almost motherly.

The doctor nodded. "It was an accident . . . she didn't want the drugs. It just happened. She hurt her back last year. I never suspected . . . never guessed until last month. Her moods were all over the place. One night she just collapsed in my arms. Begged me to find her a fix."

"Did you?" Tally asked softly.

"No." The doctor's eyes reflected concern. "Does everyone know?"

"The police and medical examiner. And I'm sure the D.A.'s office knows," Tally replied.

"Then I guess there's no sense in trying to protect Mel any longer." The doctor tried to make her voice sound careless.

"Meaning what?" Cid asked.

"My car," Rebecca began slowly, "was at our house the night Melinda was murdered. I left the lab at eight forty-five and drove home. Mel had called me earlier in the evening. She seemed happy and lighthearted. She'd decided to kick her habit." The doctor paused, fighting to control her emotions. "We have a cabin at Tahoe. She wanted us to go up there together. I agreed. I figured if she got into trouble I could take her to the local hospital. She was so sure of herself. I called Mel's floor supervisor as soon as I got off the phone and made arrangements for a thirty-day emergency leave. I was going to speak with the medical director in the morning to secure my own leave."

"Why did you go home?" Tally asked.

"To tell her how proud I was of her decision." Rebecca's tone was tinged with regret. "You must understand, our relationship was strong, but the last few weeks had been troubled."

"And when you got home?"

"She was asleep, so I headed back to the lab."

Tally gave her a suspicious smile. "I don't think so. Blood and tissue samples taken from under Melinda's nails say otherwise." Tally pointed at the doctor's right arm and the two fresh pink scars.

Rebecca Toliver's nerves tingled. "I'm not purposely trying to deceive you; I'm well aware of the evidence against me. You didn't let me finish. I was in the car, about halfway back to the hospital, when Mel called me on my car phone. She was more in a drug stupor than awake and her words were slurred. I knew she'd shot up again. She apparently had heard me leave. I went back to the house to make sure she was okay. I wanted her drugs. She wouldn't give them to me. We had a violent argument. She didn't know what she was saying, much less what she was doing. Finally she fell back on her pillow and drifted off to sleep. I covered her and kissed her forehead."

Rebecca looked up, her face a mask of sadness. "That was the last time I saw her alive. The digital clock in my car read 10:18 when I headed back to the hospital. I sat in the storage room next to the lab for about half an hour before going back to work. I needed time to think . . . time to figure out how I was going to get Melinda the treatment she needed."

Tally pulled her cramped legs from under the table and stood in the corner of the small room. "Let me see if I've got this straight. You left the hospital at eight forty-five. How long did it take you to drive home?"

"Ten minutes."

"So you arrived, give or take a few minutes, at nine o'clock?"

"Yes."

"How long were you home before you left the first time?"

"No more than ten minutes."

Cid took over. "So you were back in your car by quarter after nine?"

"Yes."

"Tell me," Cid continued, "how long did it take before you returned home after Melinda's phone call?"

The doctor sighed. "I was back in our house at nine thirty exactly. Our grandfather clock was chiming when I walked in."

"So," Tally said, bending over the table, "you were home roughly forty-five minutes?"

"Yes."

"Did you lock the door when you went into the house?"

The doctor thought for a second. "No, I shoved the door with my cane. In fact, when I went to leave, the door was standing open about three or four inches."

Cid glanced at Tally, then back to the doctor. "Did you notice anything out of the ordinary when you left?"

"Not really." The doctor raised an eyebrow. "Wait, I do remember smelling peppermint. I thought it odd because I knew Melinda had not eaten at home and we seldom have candy in the house."

Tally abruptly stopped taking notes. "You're sure you smelled peppermint?"

"Yes."

All at once, Cid felt certain that Melinda Morgan had kept many secrets from Rebecca Toliver. But there was no way to confront this one. "Why would someone kill Melinda?"

"I can't think of a reason."

"What about payment for drugs?" Cid demanded.

The doctor shook her head. "She didn't hang around with low-lifes."

"The drugs came from somewhere," Cid said condescendingly.

"Melinda was a good person," the doctor answered, focusing on Tally. "She had a kind word for everyone. And she was so full of compassion. Whether someone was hurting emotionally or was physically injured, she made that person feel that their problem was unique. That she truly cared. There is a box of letters in the bedroom closet at home from the families of past patients. The letters are a testament to her goodness. Read them, then you'll know who Melinda really was. Don't destroy her memory by making her life cheap."

"What about Dr. Spencer Jewell?" Tally's voice was neutral.

"He was Mel's doctor."

"For how long?"

"Since she hurt her back."

"Did you know anything about him? Did you check with your colleagues to see how he rated as a physician?"

Rebecca Toliver gazed at Tally. Her brown eyes were defensive. "I didn't like him, didn't like what I found out about his practice."

"Did you and Melinda discuss his medical ethics?"

"No. It was a closed subject as far as she was concerned. She never saw his faults."

Cid's eyes met the doctor's. "You knew she was using long ago."

The doctor's body stiffened, but she said nothing.

"And your relationship?" Tally probed.

"As I said earlier, the past few weeks had been difficult. But that doesn't mean our feelings, our love, had diminished any." The doctor's face was tight with grief. "I loved Melinda and she loved me. We would have spent the rest of our lives together."

Perspiration glistened at Tally's hairline. "I'm trying to follow this, but I confess I'm having a damn hard time understanding both your reasoning and your own ethics. Your lover had a drug problem . . . for what . . . almost a year, and you stood back and did nothing. A colleague was pushing drugs and you didn't report him." Outrage was brewing under the surface, and Tally was finding it nearly impossible to keep her feelings hidden.

"That's my cross to bear," the doctor answered, her voice remorseful. "Whether you believe it or not, I did what I thought was best for Melinda. If I had forced her into treatment, it would have been wasted time and energy. An addict can only be helped when he or she is ready. As for Dr. Jewell, he has been brought before the medical board on charges twice in the past five years. He was found innocent both times." She took a deep, weary breath. "I did my homework, Ms. McGinnis. Dr. Jewell has powerful friends. Despite what society may think, drug addiction is not limited to the poor and undereducated."

"Did you bring Melinda a rose the night of her death?" Cid asked abruptly.

The doctor seemed surprised by the question. "No." She shook her head vehemently. "Absolutely not. Mel hated cut flowers. She saw so many at the hospital, saw them die so quickly. She believed flowers belonged to the earth and should blossom and die a natural death."

Hands on the table, Cid raised her eyes. "Melinda's earlobes were whacked off after she was iced—any idea why?"

Dr. Toliver blanched. "As I told the police, she was wearing gold seal earrings . . ." Her hands rose in entreaty. "She would have given the earrings to anyone, if they'd asked."

"Anything special about these earrings?"

"Mel said they were made by some local artisan. I don't recall the name. They were striking. Paper thin gold with incredible detail. Obviously expensive. Not something you would buy from a street vendor. They were a gift from a former patient. As lovely as they were, the earrings certainly weren't worth Mel's life."

"You said paper thin, gold, seal earrings?" Cid questioned.

Dr. Toliver nodded.

"Name Gertrude Allendale mean anything to you? Makes earrings. Custom design. Seals are her specialty."

"No," the doctor answered.

Thoughtfully, Cid played with her pack of Virgina Slims, while making a few mental notes.

"What about strangers?" Tally asked. "Did you notice anyone hanging around the house?"

"No."

"Why did Melinda have a gun?" Tally softly asked.

The hurt in Rebecca Toliver's eyes deepened. "I gave it to her. I'm gone most of the night. I was concerned for her safety." She stared out the window at the guard. "I guess when someone's intent is to harm, having a weapon doesn't always help."

"Pacific Heights isn't an area normally associated with crime. Especially murder. Was there someone you or Melinda particularly feared?" Tally questioned.

The doctor shook her head.

Tally leaned forward, her eyes hard. "Does Johnny Lee still have a key to your house?"

Rebecca Toliver's face looked tighter. "No. I asked for it back last month."

"But he moved out a year and a half ago. Why did you wait so long?"

"It wasn't a priority."

"So he could have made a copy?"

"I suppose."

Glancing at Rebecca, Cid took out a cigarette and let it dangle from her mouth. "Is house cleaning one of your specialities? You know, something you do after you've had a violent argument with your lover?"

Rebecca folded her arms. "What are you talking about?"

"Apparently, in the middle of your despair and deep concern for Melinda, you found it necessary to mop the entry floor."

The anger in the doctor's eyes was close to total abhorrence. "As I was leaving I noticed the mud on the floor in the foyer. I don't know about you, Detective, but I was raised to clean up after myself."

Her expression curious, Tally asked, "So there were only your foot prints on the floor?"

Rebecca spread her hands. "I wasn't looking for footprints. Wasn't paying that close attention. I saw mud on the floor and I mopped it up."

"We need a motive, Doc." Cid explained. "Was anything missing from the house?"

"I don't know. Remember, I was arrested and taken away from my home. I haven't been there since."

Tally sat back down. "Who would want to frame you?" she asked quietly.

The doctor gave her a long, searching look. "No one."

"C'mon, Doc," Cid said skeptically. "Everyone's got enemies. You're the head of a department at a major hospital. Don't tell me you haven't ruffled a few feathers here and there."

Rebecca Toliver shook her head in frustration. "Ruffling a few feathers over a work-related problem is hardly motivation to destroy me—or for that matter to commit murder. I'm no goody-goody, but I also don't conduct my life in a way that makes enemies. Please keep an open mind."

Speaking with distaste, Tally asked, "And your lab coat—should we keep an open mind about that too?"

The doctor's voice was soft with anger. "Johnny promised . . ."

Cid contemplated Rebecca Toliver with silent amusement. "Loose lips sink ships. Self-preservation is a powerful motivator." Her eyes were steel, now. "Maybe you should have taken the plea bargain."

Rebecca Toliver stood abruptly. "Your insolence is deplorable." Her voice rose. "That was *my* blood on the lab coat, not Melinda's."

"And the blood on your scrubs?" Tally asked, with equal ferocity.

Rebecca took a moment. The pain of remembering filled the room. Quietly, she said, "It was

Melinda's blood. May God forgive me, I slapped her when she scratched me."

◻ ◻ ◻

Tally rubbed her bloodshot eyes as she waited for Cid to wrestle her bulk behind the steering wheel of the old Plymouth.

As always, the car was an environmental disaster. Styrofoam coffee cups and fast-food wrappers were the main ingredients of the car's decor.

"What do you think?" Tally asked curiously.

Cid fired up a cigarette and inhaled deeply. She looked tired as she cranked the ignition and let the car idle. "Could have something to do with drugs, but I doubt it. I don't think the doc is shooting straight. I think she's still hiding something."

"How so?"

Smoke slowly drifted from the corner of Cid's mouth. "That Johnny Lee . . . there's something odd going on there. And doesn't it seem a little strange that Toliver would know about the Cox Funeral Home and not know the director *well*? These ghoulish types, they rub elbows at conventions, hospital gatherings —any number of places. There's something crawling around in my gut that tells me Marsha Cox and Rebecca Toliver are a lot closer than the doc lets on. And another thing, the earlobes on my dash—there weren't any earrings." Her tone was relaxed, matter-of-fact.

"Knowing each other is one thing; murder's an entirely different story. Even if the profile fit—which it doesn't, by the way—what would have triggered Marsha Cox to kill Melinda?" Tally looked doubtful.

"Don't know. We're missing the connector. But mark my words, when we find it, Marsha Cox's name is going to be all over it." Cid checked her watch. "I'm heading over to the Cox Funeral Home, then I've got an appointment with Robin Stapleton at the *Examiner*. She's running an editorial in today's edition about Marsha Cox and the Dorset murder. I talked to her last night: she owed me a favor. Besides, Robin's been putting an article together for more than a year: something about San Francisco nobility and how the younger generation is destroying the aristocracy, or some such bullshit. I figure a story about Cox might flush her out of hiding."

"The evidence doesn't suggest . . ." This time it was Tally who let her words hang. "Just drop me by my car."

9

Tuesday, July 7
12:51 P.M.

Nestled amidst a small cluster of oak trees, the
Morgan Cox Funeral Home sat just behind the Mark
Hopkins and Fairmount Hotels on the peak of Nob Hill.
Morgan Jr. inherited the family business and sizable
fortune in 1955. He died in 1983, leaving his daughter,
Marsha, financially secure, with a thriving business and
an enviable stock portfolio.

Sandwiched between a black Lexus and bronze
Cadillac DeVille, Cid's Plymouth stuck out like a sore
thumb in the parking lot at the rear of the mortuary.

The leafy arms of oak trees encircled the sunny
afternoon and cast eerie shadows that danced on the
gray pavement as Cid made her way to the front
entrance.

For over thirty years, cruelty and death had been
part of her job, but like most everyone else, Cid found
entering a funeral home unnerving. Mournful organ
music and the oversweet smell of gardenias only added
to her discomfort. But there was no getting around
this—she had to know for herself if Marsha Cox had
contacted anyone. Experience told her fidelity could be
bought, and Marsha Cox had the bucks to buy loyalty
by the truckload.

She was grateful when out of the shadows, a rather tall man appeared. Dressed in a conservative blue suit, with a plain navy tie, Wallace Pruitt was the acting funeral director.

"Attorneys are handling the entire process," he was saying after formal introductions were made. "The Cox name is forever tainted after this distasteful act of butchery perpetrated by Marsha. As of yet, the legalities haven't been completed, but out of respect to our distinguished and privileged clientele we've moved forward and are now calling the mortuary Nob Hill Chapel. It is much easier on the families of our departed guests."

Hardly listening to Wallace Pruitt, Cid's eyes scanned the entry. She half expected Marsha Cox to walk through the door.

With his white hands folded in front of him as if in prayer, the funeral director bent slightly at the waist and asked politely, "What exactly is it I can do for you?"

From her years of training, Cid knew to keep her demeanor mild. "I'm looking for Marsha Cox, or any clue that might point me in her direction."

The funeral director's high cheekbones and thin lips twitched. "This is a place of grieving, not a hunting ground for savages. I'm sure your visit is well intended, Ms. Cameron, but we have a funeral in an hour and I really must ask that you leave."

"How 'bout a quick tour, Wally?"

"Oh, no." Wallace Pruitt raised his hands as if horrified. "We protect the privacy of our precious clients, and please, my name is Wallace."

"It's the staff," Cid continued with authority, "that I'm interested in seeing. Perhaps someone might have heard from Marsha . . ."

"Heavens no!" Wallace Pruitt interrupted. "No one, and I repeat, no one on my staff would have anything to do with that Cox woman. You must understand," he continued, nearly pleading, "we were relieved when Marsha disappeared. All of us disliked her; many of us hated her lack of professionalism here at the mortuary. And all of us feared her. She was mean-spirited, and I personally am not surprised by her wicked actions. As I've indicated, we have all spoken to the police and have nothing further to add."

Cid held his gaze, frustrated that she didn't have a police badge to thrust in his face. "I understand what you're saying, but it's human nature to forget small facts that could turn out to be an important clue to finding Marsha."

He shook his head. "There is very little about Marsha Cox that any of us will ever forget."

Cid watched him, silent. She realized that for someone like Wallace Pruitt there were no gray areas. He was a snob, yet a caring man, who lived by the rules and never strayed from the parameters of decency. He would know his staff well, not only because it was part of his job, but because they respected him and allowed him to know their most private secrets and thoughts. Cid's gaze was relentless, her arms crossed on her chest, her legs spread wide as if daring Wallace Pruitt to remove her from the funeral home.

He stood erect, nearly at attention, and glanced at his watch. When he looked up Cid saw resignation in his eyes. "As strange as it may seem," he said, "Rosa Garcia, our cleaning lady, was befriended by Marsha Cox. It was an odd pairing, given their different social status and all, but I often heard them chatting together. The police interviewed Rosa maybe a month ago. I was there and she said she knew nothing, but should you wish, you're welcome to speak with her. You'll find a door out back labeled 'Offices.' She'll be cleaning inside. Please make it brief," he added, smugly. His veiled attempt to get rid of Cid did not fool her.

Inwardly, Cid winced; she liked calling her own shots and hated the idea of being dismissed by this controlling man.

"Tell me, Wally, who's to say Marsha's not hiding here somewhere?" She pointed to the chapel and several offices down the hall.

Pruitt's brown eyes were shadowed with disapproval. "Not a chance." He pointed to the right. "The staff lunch room, the embalming quarters, my office, and the casket showroom. The door to the left leads to the crematorium, an area even Marsha found too hot to handle." It was the first suggestion that Wallace Pruitt had a sense of humor.

"And the offices out back?" Cid asked.

"Marsha's domain. I was rarely invited into her circle." Pruitt assumed an almost mournful look. "Ten minutes with Rosa, Ms. Cameron; our funeral will be assembling shortly."

Rosa Garcia was much younger than Cid expected. She was full-figured, dark, and quite pretty.

"I know nothing," she said, as Cid gently asked questions. "Marsha, she was good to me. It made the others jealous. But I was not her friend, only her employee." She smoothed the cloth on her long green skirt and shyly looked at the floor.

"What are the chances Marsha would come to your house," Cid asked, "you know, for a short stay?"

Rosa looked up, her black eyes saucers. "Never. Mama and Papa just came to San Francisco from Guadalajara two months ago. They are very old, very frail. There is no room for anyone else." She stared at Cid, her eyes pleading. "I need my job for my family; to suggest such a thing could jeopardize my position."

Cid watched her. "Marsha has to be staying somewhere, Rosa." Her voice was hard. "I know this is none of my business, but it seems to me if your parents are elderly and frail, they'd find it difficult to work. How is it they could afford a trip to San Francisco?"

Total terror crossed Rosa's face. She shook her head. "I saved the money."

Cid was silent. She ran her hand across a handsome walnut bookcase filled with rare science books, the wisdom of embalming passed down through the generations. She turned and stared coldly at Rosa. "Don't jerk me around."

Rosa's dark eyes became quite still. Her mouth felt dry. "You have no authority here."

Cid scowled, her voice determined, yet soft. "You're right, no damn authority, but I've seen Marsha's victims, Rosa, and it ain't pretty. Bodies beaten up until the flesh barely hangs on the bones and blood—"

"All right!" she screamed. "Marsha gave me the money! But months ago, and I swear I have not seen her. She knew I missed my family. Mama had been sick. I was scared she would die before I saw her again. Marsha's mother died when she was a young girl. She understood grief and gave me the money to bring my family here. Everyone thinks Marsha is bad, but she has good, too."

Cid's look was guarded. "You're playing with fire, Rosa. Sickos like Cox don't give money away without expecting something in return. I'd buy an extra lock for my door if I were you. And I'd make damn sure I wasn't out on the streets after dark."

Cid looked around the room. It was decorated in shades of gold, with plush area rugs. A brown leather couch sat smartly against one wall. "Could Cox be sleeping here at night?" she asked.

"No." Rosa stared at the couch, her hands shaking as she clutched them to her lips. "There was dust on the cushions today when I cleaned. Air-conditioning dust," she added, as if validating her cleaning skills.

Cid motioned with her hand. "What about up front in one of the other offices?"

"Oh, no. Mr. Pruitt has someone here twenty-four hours a day to receive the deceased. He says Nob Hill aristocrats don't want commoners to handle their precious dead."

"Precious dead, huh? Well, I sure as hell don't want Mr. Pruitt poking my flab when I kick the bucket." Cid glanced around the area. "What's in there?" She pointed to a small adjoining room.

"Storage for Marsha's climbing gear. The police checked last time they were here. It's just a large closet. There is no room to hide or sleep."

In the hall, a light came on. Wallace Pruitt abruptly appeared. "I'm sorry, Ms. Cameron, our guests are arriving; you'll have to leave."

"Convenient entry, Pruitt. Where's that lead to?" Cid asked, ignoring his invitation to leave.

Wallace Pruitt looked at her sharply. His voice was low. "The chapel. Years ago, when Mr. Cox was still alive, this area was used for the families of the departed. They could grieve privately, yet still hear the service. The building was remodeled shortly after his death."

Cid walked down the short hall. The organ music was louder than before. "And this," she said, pointing at another door, "where does it go?"

He raised his finger to his lips. "Shhh. Keep your voice down," he whispered. "Storage for our pine boxes. Not something we use very often on Nob Hill; still, we do get an occasional odd request every now and then. Leads underground back to the rose garden."

"Rose garden? I didn't see any roses when I came in," Cid said, surprised.

"Mrs. Cox, Marsha's mother, had a large garden at the back of the property before her death. It's hidden from view by the obelisk and memorial park. I wanted the roses removed and the parking area expanded, but Marsha wouldn't hear of it. Mrs. Cox's ashes were spread among the roses when she died. Marsha believed the soil was sacred."

Cid raised an eyebrow and then pointed at the door. "Police check this?" she asked.

"Yes. First time they were here. No one likes to go down there. Its walls are not reinforced. It's the last place I'd want to be if there was a strong earthquake."

"Any electricity?"

"Yes, and heat. It wouldn't do to have the wooden caskets mildew, now would it?"

Cid opened the door and flicked on a single, exposed lightbulb. She turned, her voice muted. "Is there an outside entrance to this?"

Wallace Pruitt shifted uncomfortably. "Yes. It hasn't been used for years. Not since Mrs. Cox was still alive and had a gardener tending to her roses."

Cid withdrew her 9mm from under her jacket. "There's a stakeout car in front of the mortuary. If someone used this rose garden door, would the police see them?"

Wallace Pruitt leaned against the wall to steady himself. "No. The door is set into a mound of dirt. Mr. Cox didn't want the peaceful view obstructed. It's doubtful most visitors or mourners even know of the door's existence."

Cid's eyes darted down the worn wooden stairs and onto the shadowed floor. Only a small bead of perspiration, caught in the wrinkle of her brow, betrayed her intense concentration. She took each step as if it might be her last. Her hand was steel as her gun swept a slow path across the empty coffins. She saw the sleeping bag first, then the garbage can filled with fast food wrappers. A hasp on the inside of the back door had been pried open.

"Call 9-1-1, Wally. Tell them to send Inspector Barney Hampton out here fast!"

"I have a funeral," he protested.

Cid looked at him hard. "I said, call 9-1-1 *Now!*"

With cold eyes she regarded Rosa. "And you . . . tell your mama and papa I sure as hell hope they enjoy their visit."

10

Tuesday, July 7
1:23 P.M.

The time-and-temperature sign on the front of the
Bank of America building read a suffocating ninety-
eight degrees.

Tally pulled her arms free of her denim shirt,
revealing a pastel blue tank top. She threw the shirt in
the back seat as she maneuvered through traffic, down
Montgomery and across Market Street to the freeway
entrance at the corner of Harrison and Fourth.

Horns honked and the sound of screeching tires
made the highway feel like a battle zone. The heat was
obviously pushing some drivers' personal thermostats
into the red zone. She was relieved when she reached
the outskirts of the city and headed south on 101 to the
Hillsborough exit.

Tally had punched up Grayson Chandler's
phone number as soon as Cid had dropped her off at
the office. Dr. Chandler was a longtime family friend, as
well as a renowned psychiatrist and criminologist. His
specialty was creating profiles of international
criminals.

The instant Grayson's wife, Carol Ann, heard
Tally's voice on the telephone she extended an
enthusiastic invitation to a family barbecue.

"You're sure I won't be imposing?" Tally had asked, after learning that Grayson was home for a week's vacation from his lucrative psychiatric practice.

"You come immediately," Carol Ann had gushed.

As Tally drove toward the Chandlers', she reflected on her long association with them. The Chandlers had begun socializing with Patrick and Victoria McGinnis early in Grayson's career. So Tally and the doctor had been acquaintances since her adolescence, and friends since her mid twenties.

Dr. Chandler was a big, jovial man who sported a pretentious goatee and loved pricey wine and good food. Carol Ann was active in a dozen charities, but most of her time and devotion was spent on her Japanese garden. The Chandlers lived in Hillsborough, a small community long inhabited by rich and successful families such as the Hearsts, Bing Crosby's widow, and many other celebrities.

As Tally drove down the long driveway that led to the Chandler estate, she was glad she had taken Carol Ann up on her invitation. Tall redwoods shaded the parklike grounds, and green ferns hid the rich black earth.

Twin black Lincoln Town Cars were parked outside a six-bay garage, along with a green Geo and a sixties-vintage Volkswagen van. Tally knew the van belonged to Grayson's son, who was in a doctorate program at Berkeley, and she guessed that the Geo belonged to the Chandlers' daughter, also a student at Berkeley.

Mrs. Chandler strode across the lawn toward Tally, her arms open wide. Her Guess jeans, cut off above the knee, and a bright orange cotton shirt tied just below her breasts gave the impression of a woman much younger than sixty-two. "Tally, my sweetness, it's been so long."

Carol Ann, taller than Tally by a full three inches, wrapped her long arms around her guest and hugged her with genuine warmth.

Tally greeted her with equal enthusiasm.

When Carol Ann drew back, looking at Tally's face with mild alarm, she said, "Looks like work is a little rough on your anatomy."

Tally smiled, but said nothing.

Looping her arm through Tally's, Carol Ann guided her down a wide, hedge-lined path toward the pool and patio. "I had lunch with your mother last week. Seems the older we get the less time we spend with our friends. Your mother is such a gracious woman."

Tally raised an eyebrow and grinned impishly. "I'm not sure I would describe Mother as gracious."

Carol Ann's tanned nose wrinkled as she snorted and chuckled. "If I were being totally honest I'm not sure that I would characterize Victoria as gracious, either, but then not many people would use such a term to portray most of us." Carol Ann chuckled again as she squeezed Tally's arm.

"I've missed seeing you," Tally said emphatically, her green eyes bright.

"Victoria is crushed because you haven't asked her to join you on a cruise I believe you are going on soon."

Tally stopped in her tracks and stifled a laugh. "Carol Ann, it's a lesbian cruise. Mother may be open to my lifestyle, but I fear to think what she might do surrounded by five-hundred loving female couples."

They both laughed at the thought.

"And I hear there's new love in your life," Carol Ann noted.

"Her name is Katie O'Neil and she's a blue-eyed brunette from Ireland. She's lived in the United States for eight years and worked for me for the past seven.

She's a full partner now at the agency." Tally hesitated, then said thoughtfully, "I can't believe I worked with her all these years and never saw her, never really knew her. We're taking it slowly. But I love her." She quickly glanced at her watch. It was well after one o'clock and she hadn't called to cancel her lunch date with Katie. All signs of playfulness disappeared from her face.

Carol Ann looked keenly at her. "I'm happy for you."

Grayson Chandler waved a long-handled spatula over his head in greeting. "Welcome to nature's poetry lesson," he said, sounding every bit the academic.

Tally moved forward to say hello. Grayson's ample girth protruded from under his white apron and his chef's hat sat tilted on his head; Tally couldn't help thinking as she crossed the patio that he looked like the Pillsbury Doughboy. "The hamburgers smell wonderful," she said, pecking the doctor on his cheek.

Grayson pulled a bottle of Dow's 1977 vintage porto from the outdoor bar next to the barbecue. "Wine?"

"Just a taste," she answered, her thumb and finger indicating a small amount. "I'm driving and, unfortunately, working."

Dr. Chandler looked over Tally's shoulder at his wife. "And you, dear?"

"Not just now. I'll leave the two of you alone to chat. Perhaps Tally can come back for a longer visit when she's off duty."

Grayson poured two inches of the red liquid into a tall crystal glass and passed it to Tally as he looked at her questioningly.

Her face clouded. "I need help."

He nodded. "I suspected as much when my office faxed the information your secretary had sent them." He carefully brushed a rich brown sauce onto the hamburgers, shut the lid on the gas grill, and turned down the burners. "Shall we sit?"

Tally followed the doctor to an alcove in the corner of the patio, taking a seat in a flowery canvas chair. She sipped her wine.

"Your notes were limited. I'm not sure whether I can provide much help." He drank the last of his wine, allowing the liquid to linger on his palate before he swallowed.

"I've only been on the case one day, and unfortunately, the D.A. is looking for info from my client's attorney by one o'clock tomorrow."

Grayson stroked his goatee. "I won't stake my reputation on this. For me to be more accurate I'd need pictures and data. However, it appears the Morgan murder was cold and calculating. I don't sense rage here; the motive was more likely to have involved indignity or hurt—perhaps a rejected lover. You believe a woman committed this crime?"

"The evidence seems to suggest that."

"I would agree. A woman, or perhaps a mama's boy. The mode of death is exact and calm, meaning the wounds were precise and the body trauma was limited to the cause of death. Bullies or men trying to project their manliness will normally leave bruises on the victim, either from beating or squeezing: a literal externalization of power. I've mentioned in the past that generally a man releases his rage more directly simply by cutting the victim's throat, for example, or stabbing her repeatedly."

"But Melinda Morgan's throat was cut," Tally protested.

"Yes, but in this case there's an element of precision." Dr. Chandler swiped at the air with his empty wineglass, as if slashing something. "That's vicious." He brought the wineglass to his throat and made a quick jerking motion. "That's precision and neatness, suggesting compulsive organization. There's no mention in your paperwork that any vital neck arteries were cut."

"No, just the windpipe."

Tally was silent for a time. "What about the earlobes?"

"That's a power stroke: your killer's signature."

She shivered.

"As for the second crime, the woman in the park, it sounds remarkably like the case you brought me a couple of months ago. Tremendous rage and someone who's fearless. Or more accurately, reckless in her actions toward others. The two crimes carry the same compulsive organization and neatness; that is, the body stretched out to form a cross, the arterial tube in the femoral artery, and the rose."

"I don't believe this is the same perpetrator," Tally declared, her voice filled with anxiety. "Where's the thrill? Last time Marsha Cox brought her victim down the side of a mountain. The whole scenario was dashing and daring. This time she simply laid the body in a clearing. No opportunities for glory. It doesn't fit."

"Sorry, Tally, the signature's the same: Cox abuses her victims after they are dead. I believe she's a serial killer. Her M.O. would change over time, but never the signature."

"But why wasn't Melinda Morgan abused? And why was she killed indoors?"

"I'd say it happened indoors because the element of risk was higher; the chance of getting caught was greater. The park is, for the most part, deserted. Neighbors tend to be nosy and interruption or discovery is much greater in a home. Her satisfaction level would be soaring. She could have been interrupted before she started the act of abuse. That would account for the second killing in the park. She returned to the last place she was successful, where she controlled everything: all the elements, all the players. She's feeling more pressure now. She must intensify her crimes to get any satisfaction. With the pressure will come a feeling of loss of control. With the loss of control—"

"More people will be killed," Tally interrupted.

"Exactly, and returning to the park boosted the thrill. She knew there would be police patrols, maybe undercover officers in the brush. This time she achieved satisfaction, but as the pressure builds, the feeling of loss of control will grow. More heinous crimes will follow."

"She's taunting us, daring us to catch her," Tally said heatedly. "The earlobes turned up on the dashboard of Cid's car."

"Are you surprised at that? She's clever and she's getting away with murder," Grayson responded crisply.

Dr. Chandler rose from his chair and walked to the bar, where he carefully refilled his wineglass, breathing in the bouquet before taking a sip. "Marsha Cox appears to have a tremendous ego. If she was interrupted while killing the Morgan woman, I suspect she left a marker: something that would identify her as the killer. Not just the earlobes. Something the police wouldn't ordinarily pick up. A peculiarity of some sort, that gave her a minuscule amount of pleasure." The doctor took another sip of wine. "Look carefully, my friend, and be careful. You're still trying to apply logic to this murderer's thought processes, and it doesn't work. If you push her, she will act."

Tally felt her body stiffen. "Cid has arranged for an editorial to appear in the afternoon edition of the *Examiner*. She figured it would flush Marsha Cox out of hiding."

"If she's not escalating and is under control, she'll attack in her own time." Grayson removed his chef's hat and rubbed the bald spot on the back of his graying head. "If this profile applies, and my professional experience suggests it does, the article will flush her out." He paused, again stroking his goatee. "Police logic, how shall I say . . . is not always a thoughtful process. The profile of the murderer that we have discussed is only a limited guess. Without complete information I cannot be sure Marsha Cox is the killer in *this* case; however, flushing a known killer from hiding is a deadly game—and one that will only serve the murderer's desire. Personally, I'd say the newspaper article is a foolish mistake that could be very costly."

11

Tuesday, July 7
4:21 P.M.

After parking in front of a mom-and-pop grocery store on the outskirts of Hillsborough, Tally picked up a copy of the *Examiner* and rushed back to her car. As she flipped through the newspaper, the promised editorial jumped out at her.

A Coward's Story
By Robin Stapleton, Editor

As one of the privileged few who have lived the aristocratic lifestyle of the Nob Hill set, Marsha Cox would seem to be an unlikely candidate for the role of serial killer. Yet, on a fog-shrouded May night, after an evening of sexual pleasures, Cathy Dorset, a young soon-to-be multimillionaire, was viciously murdered. Although never brought to trial, Marsha Cox confessed to the killing before escaping capture. Last night's murder of another woman in the Little Capitan park is an eerie duplicate of the Dorset homicide.

In a ruthless world in which murder has somehow become part of our daily lives, the killings at Little Capitan stand out as examples of sociopathic cruelty and brutality: the work of a twisted, troubled mind. The act of a coward. Lock your doors, neighbors, and watch your backs—a serial killer is still at large.

Were it not for the quick action of our chief of police, his staff, and the passion of trained professionals such as former police lieutenant Cid Cameron, who are all relentlessly hunting Marsha Cox, I fear San Francisco's golden image might be forever tarnished, and its laughter silenced.

We insist that the police pull out all stops in their efforts to bring this reign of terror to an end.

◻ ◻ ◻

Tally could barely keep from cursing as she sat boxed in by commuter traffic. The freeway drive back into the city hadn't been bad, as most traffic was headed south. However, when she nosed her car into Market Street the logjam became a test of her patience and endurance.

She picked up the car phone and stabbed up Rita Cruz's number. "Are you going to be at the office long?" Tally asked when Rita came on the line.

"Twenty, thirty minutes max. Why?" the attorney asked, brisk and to the point.

"I need the keys to Rebecca Toliver's house." Tally paused. "The police did give them to you?"

"No, her former attorney turned the keys over to me the day I accepted the case. The doctor gave you signed permission to enter the house?"

"No. Do I need it?" Tally asked, feeling foolish.

"It wouldn't hurt," the attorney answered, sounding dubious. "You have to consider the liability if something is missing or broken. It's an expensive house, Tal. Stranger things have happened." Rita's voice was now neutral.

Tally glanced at her watch. "I'm running out of time . . . I'll have to take the chance. Can you leave the key for me?"

"Where are you now?"

"About four blocks away, moving three inches every time the light changes."

Laughing, Rita answered, "I'll wait. Park and run in." She wasn't kidding. "Anything new on the case?"

"Lots . . . and nothing. Cid is convinced Marsha Cox killed Melinda Morgan. Pick up today's *Examiner* and check out the editorial in section A titled "A Coward's Story." I just finished reading it. It gave me goose bumps. To call Marsha Cox a coward is as good as a declaration of war. If she reads this story, it will surely incite her."

"Cox. What pleasant news. I'm not surprised, given the rose and all. You don't buy Cid's hypothesis, I take it?" Rita asked.

"It's too soon. It's not that I'm dismissing her as a strong suspect. It's just that there *are* other possibilities. Your client, for one. She hasn't been exactly forthright, and there's a lab tech at the hospital that makes me squirm every time I think about him."

She paused and looked out the car window; for a strange moment she felt very frightened.

"Right now, the indecision you're hearing in my voice is related to the newspaper editorial. I'm afraid Cid is obsessed with Marsha Cox and isn't seeing the whole picture. That could be very costly for all concerned."

Rita Cruz swiveled in her office chair. "For sure it's costly, McGinnis, especially when you're charging me four hundred bucks an hour on this case. A little steep."

"Right," Tally answered, sounding annoyed. "I'm sorry, Rita, but without evidence to indicate otherwise, your client remains in the hot seat."

"I'll see you when you get here." The attorney's voice was softer now.

◻ ◻ ◻

After she picked up the key, Tally drove straight up Van Ness and then cut over to California Street. The traffic was lighter and her mood was much improved.

The exterior of Dr. Rebecca Toliver's three-story Edwardian on Webster Street was impressive—white stucco with polished wood inlays and crown molding. Over the years, neatly trimmed ivy had migrated across the stucco, giving the old, restored mansion a look reminiscent of academia.

Bright yellow crime-scene tape on the door had been cut weeks before, but not removed.

Tally opened the lock easily and was instantly overtaken by the beauty of the interior of the house. From the foyer she could see into the living room. The highly polished wooden beams, bookcases, and mantelpiece bore impressive testimony to the artisans and woodcraft of a previous era.

The furniture was mostly Queen Anne. The Victorian-era portraits showed stern-faced ancestors, but a few watercolors in the hall prevented the atmosphere from becoming oppressive.

As Tally wound her way through what seemed to be a maze of rooms, she was struck by the cleanliness and order of the house. There was not a footprint on the Persian rugs, or a speck of gritty dusting powder remaining from the forensics team's work. Someone had cleaned.

She rounded a corner into a shallow hallway that opened to a sunny, warm breakfast nook. Outside, window boxes filled with scarlet and purple fuchsias lined the bay windows, bringing the garden into the room.

She had taken only two steps into the room when suddenly the cold-steel business end of a double-barreled shotgun was shoved into the nape of her neck.

"May I ask what you're doing here?" The woman's voice was raspy with age.

"I work for Dr. Toliver."

"No, I don't believe that to be true." The gun was pushed deeper into Tally's flesh.

"Indirectly, I do," Tally added hastily. "I'm an investigator hired by her attorney."

"Your name?"

"Tally McGinnis."

"Do you have identification?"

"In the glove box of my car."

"How did you get into the house?"

"May I reach into the pocket of my pants?"

"Slowly."

With that, Tally produced a brass key attached to a white tag that had Rebecca Toliver's name printed in bold black letters.

The gun was lowered and Tally slowly turned around.

"Alberta Rogers," a small, frail woman said. "Please forgive my rudeness. I've been edgy ever since Melinda's passing."

With great effort she tried to set the gun against the wall, but the stock hit the floor with a resounding thud, the barrel gouging a piece of mahogany trim as it crashed to the floor.

"I'm afraid guns aren't my forte. Why anyone would want to tote such a heavy piece of armament is beyond me."

Although well into her eighties, Alberta Rogers still carried herself in a dignified manner. Her white

hair was pulled severely back from her forehead and
gathered into a small bun at the back of her head. She
was dressed in an old black Chanel suit accented by a
single strand of pearls; her ears sported matching clip-
on earrings.

"Why are you here and why wasn't I notified of
your impending visit?" Alberta asked, her hands folded
in front of her.

Tally bent, picked up the gun, and set it in a
corner behind a white wicker chair. "This is an
antique."

"Yes," the older woman answered, her gray eyes
staring intently. "It belonged to Rebecca's grandfather,
may God rest his soul. I doubt it has been fired in fifty
years. Now please answer my question."

"I didn't know I was coming myself until just a
few hours ago. I didn't have time to notify the doctor.
And to be honest, Ms. Rogers, I didn't know anyone
was living in the house. I can give you her attorney's
home number if you would like to verify who I am."

"I would like that," she answered pleasantly.

When the call was completed she looked at Tally
and smiled. "I knew you weren't lying. Your eyes
would have given you away if you were. Rebecca's like
that. I can always tell when she's stretching the truth.
I've been with her since she was a baby. First as a
nanny, then as a chaperon, and now I'm just a
doddering old woman who needs looking after. Shall
we sit?" Her gait was unsteady as she made her way to
the wicker chair.

"You live here full-time?"

"I used to travel, but it has been some years ago
now. Although my pride hates to admit it, my health
hasn't been the best."

Removing her notepad and pencil from her
pants pocket, Tally sat down in a matching wicker chair.

Gently she asked, "Were you here the night Melinda was murdered?"

Alberta stared out the window at a hummingbird feeding on a fuchsia. Her hands trembled until she clasped them together again.

"Yes. I live on the third floor, in the back of the house. A lovely solarium. The stars, the view, and, of course, my books are my companions. I take lunch with Rebecca each day, before she leaves for work. Melinda's hours varied—usually she came in late, after I was in bed. I rarely saw her except on the weekends. As I told the police, Rebecca and Melinda's suite is on the first floor, and although my hearing is quite good, no sound travels through these well-built walls. I'm afraid I neither saw nor heard anything the night of the tragedy."

"How did Rebecca and Melinda get along?"

She stared into space for a moment. "Like this," she finally answered, holding up two fingers tightly pinched together. "No question that their love for each other ran deep."

"And Johnny Lee, did you know him well?"

Alberta gave Tally a sour look. "Yes. He is not a boy I particularly like, but he is reasonably well mannered."

"What don't you like about him?"

"I don't trust him." She laughed abruptly. "But then, I don't trust many young people nowadays. Perhaps it's my age speaking rather than good judgment."

Her voice had a brittle quality as she continued. "A few years back, when my legs were still strong, I used to wander this old house at night. I imagined the parties that might have once been held here, and the dignitaries who crossed the threshold." She leaned forward. "On at least three occasions, when I was roaming about, I found Johnny Lee sitting on the floor outside of Rebecca and Melinda's bedroom, his ear pressed to the door. I'm afraid I lost all respect for the young man after that."

"Did you tell Melinda or Dr. Toliver about this?"

"Oh, yes. I spoke to Rebecca on two occasions. She didn't seem particularly troubled by the events, so after finding Johnny a third time, I decided to quit my nocturnal promenades. He moved to his own apartment a short while afterwards."

Tally stared at her. "Do you have any idea why Johnny would be listening at their door or, for that matter, what he heard?"

Alberta Rogers' smile was filled with years of wisdom. "I respect privacy. As to a motive for Johnny Lee's eavesdropping, perhaps it would be best if you spoke to him regarding that issue."

Tally smiled respectfully and changed the subject. "Would it be terribly inconvenient for you to show me where your room is in relation to Melinda's bedroom?"

"No trouble at all, my dear."

Using Tally's arm for support, Alberta Rogers made her way down another hallway Tally had yet to explore. She stopped at an intricately carved mahogany door and pushed a lighted button next to the handle. The door buzzed and opened, revealing a small elevator that had a tiny seat tucked into one corner.

"My limousine." Even in the dim light it was easy to see the playfulness in Alberta's eyes.

"Will this hold both of us?" Tally asked, helping the woman inside.

"Certainly, dear. Just shut the door and the el will automatically start its ascent."

Tally did as instructed. When they arrived at the third floor, the door buzzed and opened.

Alberta pulled herself up, waiting for Tally to exit, but she didn't move. She seemed startled.

"What is it, dear?"

Feeling the old woman's gaze, Tally turned slowly. "There are no controls inside this elevator, correct?"

Alberta seemed puzzled by Tally's question. "As you can see, none. The el is controlled by computer. I don't understand computers, but Rebecca says they are all the rage."

Tally rubbed her eyes as if very fatigued. "Bear with me for a moment." She helped the woman sit back down. "I want you to think very carefully. The night Melinda was murdered, you were in the solarium asleep, correct?"

"Yes. Well . . . off and on." She smiled. "When one gets to be my age, dear, one never does everything all the way. I usually sleep for a few hours, then get up and gaze at the stars. Some nights I read for several hours before I sleep again."

"Do you ever go downstairs?"

"Rarely. Rebecca put a small refrigerator in my room, discreetly hidden in a closet. She keeps it stocked with fruit, snacks, and little cartons of juice. I'm well looked after."

Tally rubbed her eyes again. "When you do go downstairs at night, what is the purpose?"

Alberta Rogers' cheeks flushed. "For a shot of gin."

Tally smiled at her reply. "And you're sure on the night Melinda was murdered you didn't have a little Tanqueray?"

Alberta shut the elevator door and they immediately began their descent. "Quite sure," she said, mischief in her voice. She liked showing off her contraption. "I thought about it, but I changed my mind. When you're old you can do that and not feel stupid. It was raining outside and this big, old house gets damp and creaky. I decided to seek the warmth of my electric blanket instead."

The elevator came to a stop and the door opened. Tally knelt down so that her eyes were even with Alberta's. "On that horrible night, did you open the elevator door in the solarium to come downstairs?"

"Yes," the old woman smiled. "There was a terrible draft."

"So, when you shut the door, the elevator would have made its descent downstairs with no one in it and the door would have opened automatically?"

"The door would have buzzed, but not opened without someone sitting on the seat. What are you getting at?"

Tally ignored the question. "Do you know about what time that could have been?"

"Certainly, dear. I looked at the clock just before I pulled the covers over my head. It was ten thirty-five." Alberta's voice held a trace of panic. "Have I done something wrong?"

Tally took the old woman's hands in hers. "No. You did everything right." She thought for a moment. "Rebecca and Melinda's bedroom is just down the hall from the elevator?"

"Why, yes. How did you know?"

"Just a lucky guess. I need to have a look around down here. I want to see the bedroom. Thank you for all of your help."

"You don't need to see the solarium? It won't be an imposition."

"Not this time. I'll make sure I lock up when I'm done. Is there anything I can get you . . . maybe a shot of Tanqueray?"

Alberta Rogers motioned with her hand for Tally to come closer, as if someone other than Tally might hear her. "Frankly, dear, I like the bathtub variety best."

Rebecca and Melinda's bedroom was attractively decorated in tones of pale pink and deep rose.

Tally paused in front of a pastel portrait of a beautiful young woman. The clean lines and angles of Melinda Morgan's face held both innocence and compassion. Her smoky-blue eyes were alive and smiling. In that instant Tally connected with something in Melinda Morgan's eyes. In the next instant she felt cheated that she would never know Melinda except through the memories of others.

Tally turned reluctantly to face the room. Only the box spring remained on the king-size bed. The mattress had been removed either by the police or by whoever did the housecleaning. The headboard was an antique Queen Anne replica made to fit the king-size frame. One of the drawers in the Queen Anne table, next to the bed, also was missing. Otherwise the room was neat and orderly. No dusting powder or blood could be seen.

Grayson's words echoed in her head. *"This woman has a tremendous ego. If she was interrupted while killing Morgan, I suspect she left a mark, something that would identify her as the killer."*

Tally's eyes scanned the walls and floors, looking for anything obvious. She saw nothing unusual. She checked the bathroom and the closets, then checked them again. Still nothing.

Exiting the bedroom through a door on the opposite side of the room from where she had come in, Tally found the wicker basket just down the hall. The container looked out of place. She guessed it was used for dirty clothes and had never been returned to the laundry.

She discovered a closet a few feet from where the wicker basket sat. "This is where you hid, you bastard," Tally whispered, the hair on the back of her neck and arms standing on end. She opened the door slowly, knowing no one was there. Still, she sensed a presence, guessed at the panic Melinda Morgan must have felt.

A tan London Fog trench coat, three pairs of black ski pants, and a bright blue skin diving suit were hanging in the closet. No ghosts waited, no shadows lurked. On the floor sat two pairs of Lands' End hiking boots and a ragged pair of moccasins. Nothing looked out of place.

Checking the coat pockets, she found only Kleenex. Next she searched under and inside the shoes, then the moccasins. In the heel of the right moccasin she found a small piece of paper, similar to a gum wrapper. The torn bit of blue paper showed a few letters printed in white. The only visible letters were "MS" about a quarter of an inch tall, and the very small letters "RE" directly below. The rest of the words had been torn away. She held the paper to her nose; it smelled of peppermint.

12

Tuesday, July 7
7:45 P.M.

Tally wearily drove her car down Broadway. The waterfront lay to her left; the sun was just beginning its sizzling descent into the Pacific. By the time she pulled into the parking garage at the Phoenix Detective Agency she was tired and anxious to debrief with both Cid and Katie. She retrieved a bottle of Sebastiani white zinfandel that Grayson had sent along, and headed for the elevator.

Katie was still working at her computer when Tally opened the door, and she glanced up with a startled expression. "Well," she said, her brogue thick, "I was thinkin' I might be the only person workin' here any longer." Her radiant smile was beautiful in the early-evening light.

Tally moved to stand beside her. "Peace offering?" She held up the bottle of wine. "I'm sorry about lunch."

"Aye, and the phone in your car is still broken?"

Tally set the bottle of wine on the desk and reached out to embrace Katie.

Katie's mouth was warm.

"Da always said, 'Good things are worth waitin' for.' How was your day?" she asked, cupping Tally's face in her hands.

"Long, and not over yet. Cid here?"

Katie shook her head. "No. She called. Said she was havin' dinner with Barney Hampton and to call her on the car phone if you need her." Katie's jaw tightened. "Cid has found evidence Marsha's been stayin' in a seldom-used storage room at the funeral home."

Stunned, Tally murmured, "But she didn't find Marsha?"

"No."

"I was so sure Marsha was on the lam. Cid was right all along." The statement gave Tally pause: *Maybe Marsha Cox did kill Melinda Morgan.*

Tally glanced at her watch. "What I need is a quick shower and change of clothes. I want to link up with Harry before he leaves the lab."

Katie stepped back, unable to hide her disappointment.

"But first—" Tally looked at the bottle of wine and then at Katie— "how 'bout we take a few minutes up on the roof. We can watch the sunset while I catch you up?"

Surprise and pleasure, warm and sudden, flashed across Katie's face. "Here?" she asked, her blue eyes wide.

"Of course." Tally felt herself grinning. "You get the glasses, I'll uncork the wine."

Tally stood gazing at the Golden Gate Bridge, its orange towers blazing in the setting sun. The feathered ends of her strawberry-blonde hair fluttered in the breeze. The few freckles that dotted her straight nose were more pronounced in the evening light. Her green eyes seemed far away as she waited for Katie to pour the wine.

What was the connector? What was the motive? Was it possible Marsha Cox, a serial killer, could have randomly killed Melinda Morgan? She shook her head absently and said aloud, "Doesn't make sense."

"What doesn't make sense?" Katie asked, setting a glass of zinfandel atop the low wall that enclosed the roof's perimeter.

Tally picked up her glass and moved next to Katie, placing a gentle kiss upon her neck. "I don't know, my sweet Katie. This whole business of murder and Marsha Cox and dead bodies. Whatever made me choose such a profession? I must be crazy."

Katie linked her arm through Tally's. "Because you're good at what you do, my love." Her blue eyes were still and serious. "I read the article in the *Examiner*. It scared me. Brought back too many old memories of Marsha. The woman is mad."

For a moment their eyes locked in silent recollection. Katie withdrew her arm from Tally's and leaned over to look down at the street. The sidewalks were almost black in the building's shadow. From twenty stories up, the people and cars below looked like toy versions of themselves. She abruptly straightened and turned to Tally. "Promise me, you *will* be careful?"

Tally nodded. They stood in silence, watching the sun dip deeper into the Pacific until it was only a pool of light on the water. Tally gazed at the sky and then at Katie, whose hair looked nearly black as the lights of the city became brighter and the sky darker. For a very few precious moments all that mattered was the love she felt for this beautiful woman.

"By the way, I called South Carolina," Katie said, shattering the moment. "Johnny Lee is no innocent."

Tally was instantly alert. "Go on," she prodded.

"He ran away from home at the age of twelve and was picked up a week later after tryin' to hold up a gas station with a BB gun."

Katie sat down on a small, wooden bench and set her glass of wine next to her. "The judge released him into the custody of an elderly aunt who was raisin' a foster child. From what I understand, he was as happy as a leprechaun sitting on a pot of gold livin' there."

"That's it?" Tally said, disappointedly.

"Not hardly," Katie continued as the darkness deepened. "At the age of fifteen, Johnny Lee was arrested for rape and attempted murder."

Tally's heart was pounding.

As Katie reached for her wine she inadvertently knocked over the glass, sending fragments in all directions.

Tally pulled Katie from her seat, carefully stepping over the broken glass. "Go on," she encouraged.

"The foster child who was livin' with Johnny Lee's elderly aunt? Well, seems she was a seventeen-year-old beauty that Johnny Lee took a fancy to. She rebuffed his advances and somewhere along the line things got out of hand. Charges were eventually dropped, but Johnny spent the remainder of his high school years in a juvenile reform school. At the age of eighteen he disappeared from Goose Creek and no one has seen him since."

Pacing, Tally asked, "Was the girl seriously hurt?"

"If you're meanin' physically, the answer is no. As to what emotional damage was done, I couldn't say. I did get her name. I knew you would want to call."

"Fantastic! You're sure your information is correct?"

"My instincts say yes. I found the aunt's phone number and gave her a call. She now lives in a nursin' home, but her younger sister occupies the house. It's amazin' how much information people are willin' to part with when they are made to feel important." Katie laughed. "Didn't hurt either that the sister has a love of the gossip. I tried to verify the information with the sheriff's office," she continued in her soft Irish lilt, "but because of Johnny Lee's age at the time of his arrest the records are sealed."

Smiling, Tally praised Katie. "You do good work. I'm proud of you."

Katie made a small mock curtsy, then asked seriously, "Why would Johnny Lee hurt Melinda Morgan?"

Tally knelt and began picking up pieces of glass. "I'm not sure he did." She stopped and stared out into the darkness as if looking for a light. "Just another piece of the puzzle."

"I'll get another wineglass and something to put the broken pieces of glass in. Now, be careful not to cut your lovely hands," Katie said, and crossing the roof quickly, she exited down a short stairwell to the elevator.

Tally continued to pick up fragments of glass, collecting them in the palm of her hand, when she heard the sound of footsteps on the gravel rooftop. She looked up, expecting to see Katie, but whoever it was stayed in the shadows. Suddenly alert, Tally dropped the glass shards and brushed her hand. A sliver of glass pierced her palm, but she didn't notice.

The sound of footsteps stopped. Only the wind and the blare of a car horn far below could be heard.

Except for the mercury vapor light at the entrance to the stairwell, the roof was dark. Tally continued to scan the shadows.

The crunch of gravel began again. Tally tried to follow the sound, but the wind sent it in all directions. The footsteps quickened. Still in a crouched position, Tally turned first to the left, then the right. Alarms were going off in her head. Quickly, she pulled her .38. "Who's there?" she barked.

No answer.

Time slowed to a crawl, and each fraction of a second heightened her senses. Suddenly out of the darkness, a powerful arm closed around her windpipe, cutting off her air. "Drop the gun, McGinnis, or I'll snap your pretty neck, just like a matchstick."

Reluctantly, Tally complied. The attacker kicked the gun aside, along with a spray of gravel. A cold, metal blade savagely caressed Tally's throat. Warm blood trickled down her neck and across her chest, staining her blouse. She tried to break free, but to no avail. Her attacker was strong and Tally was growing weak from lack of oxygen.

"Well, good evening, McGinnis."

The metallic voice echoed in her skull. Dimly, Tally recognized the voice. Her eyes began to cloud over as consciousness slipped away. Then, suddenly, the grip was loosened. She gasped for air. Each second brought new clarity to her thoughts. She could still feel the weight of the arm around her neck, and the knife biting into her throat.

"Altitude getting to you?" Marsha Cox's throaty voice crawled into Tally's consciousness, sending shivers up the P.I.'s spine.

"Katie . . . did you hurt her?"

"Oh, McGinnis. You *are* so gallant. I have you in the grip of death and your thoughts are only for your lover." Marsha's hatred was nakedly apparent in her voice. "Someone of greater compassion might find that touching."

Tally's mouth was dry. She waited for an opportunity to turn the tables on Marsha. She was determined not to be a victim again.

Feeling invincible, Marsha removed the knife from Tally's throat and placed it in the sheath that hung on her belt. Slowly, she moved her hand just beneath Tally's breast.

Incensed, Tally cocked her elbow and slammed it into Marsha's solar plexus. There was an audible gasp as Marsha's hand fell away from Tally's breast.

Diving left, Tally rolled onto the rooftop gravel, then quickly into a crouch. She remained motionless, too frightened to breathe. Her heart pounded out a rhythm of fear. Her eyes were riveted on the shadows surrounding her. The moonless night was not Tally's ally. *Where's my damn gun*, Tally thought.

"Frisky tonight, aren't we, McGinnis?"

Tally tried to follow Marsh Cox's voice. As her footsteps drew closer, Tally focused all of her chi. Every muscle was tensed.

She could feel the heat of Marsha's body, hear her breath between gusts of wind, but the darkness stole her exact position. *Oh, God, Katie, don't come back now.*

Tally waited. When she was sure Marsha was close enough, she sprang. Gravel spitting, shards of glass cracking. In a flash, she executed a leg sweep, followed by a thrust kick, and then a side kick. Nothing. Her legs connected with empty space. Turning too quickly, she slipped on the gravel, stumbled. Before she could regain her balance, Marsha was on her. Expertly, she wrenched Tally's head back and pushed the edge of the razor-sharp knife hard against Tally's throat. A new line of blood formed on the glistening blade. Tally stifled a rising scream.

"What do you want, you *bitch?*" Tally barely managed to whisper, her voice tight with fear.

Marsha laughed sardonically. "As if you're in a position to ask." Her lips were next to Tally's ear. She moaned softly as skin touched skin. "New perfume, McGinnis, or is that lust I smell?"

Tally squirmed, trying to break free.

"My, my, such hot pants." Marsha's tongue followed the curve of Tally's ear. Her hips pressed hard against Tally's butt. Again Marsha moaned, pulling Tally even closer.

"I read the piece in the newspaper. Flattering, don't you think? Your fat friend Cid Cameron is a newsmonger who shoves her nose where it doesn't belong. Get her off my back. Do you understand, McGinnis?" With her free hand she pulled hard on Tally's throat, nearly cutting off Tally's air supply once more.

Tally made a strangled sound of affirmation.

"You're a smart woman, McGinnis. I would've found you boring otherwise and killed you long ago. Listen carefully." Her breath was hot on Tally's ear. "I didn't kill the Morgan bitch, and I haven't been to Little Capitan recently. Someone's playing games. You find out who. If not, you'll all die . . . and I'll start with your sweet Irish lass."

Marsha tightened her grip for emphasis, until once again Tally could not breathe. "I like this little game of cat-and-mouse. Now go fetch the cheese like an obedient pet!" Slowly she swiped the edge of Tally's ear with her tongue. "Ummm, so good."

Without warning, Marsha dropped her arm and drew the knife away from Tally's neck, then shoved Tally to the ground. As Tally began to crawl, her fingers felt the barrel of her .38. Gratefully, she grabbed the gun, swung around, and fired several rounds in the direction of the fading footsteps. In spite of the pain, she jumped to her feet and ran to the stairwell, but Marsha Cox was gone.

□ □ □

It seemed an eternity before she saw the door to the Phoenix Detective Agency and stumbled forward to open it. Katie was sitting safely at her desk talking on the telephone when Tally fell into the room and collapsed in a heap on the floor. Fear had stolen the last of her strength.

Tally's face was dripping with sweat, her neck full of blood. The phone slipped from Katie's hand, hit the rug with a dull thud. She raced over to Tally. "Oh, my God."

Tally pointed at the door. "Lock it!" she ordered.

13

Tuesday, July 7
8:44 P.M.

Steam hung in the air, filling the bathroom at the detective agency and covering Tally like a protective shield. Hot water jetted into every pore. She scrubbed her skin pink, then scrubbed it again. Marsha Cox could not be washed down the drain.

Images from the rooftop struggle stole their way into the shower. Several times Tally touched her throat.

"You all right?" Cid's voice boomed off the walls. "Get out here so I can talk to you." Sudden tears appeared at the corner of Cid's eyes, surprising her. She quickly wiped her face.

Tally turned her back to the fine spray. "Relax, Cidney, I'm fine. Outside of scaring me half to death, she didn't really hurt me."

Cid swatted at the steam, cutting a path to the shower door. "According to Katie, Marsha used a knife."

"Just a couple of nicks. Blood made it look worse than it was. My neck is bruised a little."

"You trying to sound cool?"

The shower stopped abruptly. Tally pulled a green bath towel from the overhead rack, wrapped it around her, and opened the door. "No."

Grabbing a matching towel from the counter, she vigorously rubbed her hair, then wiped the mirror. She caught Cid's steamy reflection and said, "If Marsha Cox wanted me dead, I wouldn't be here right now. That's not cool; it's just plain scary."

"Your point being what?" Cid crossed her arms.

"I'm useful to her." Tally whisked a brush through her damp hair. As the feathered ends fell into place, her bangs dipped across the corner of her right eye. "She didn't kill Melinda Morgan."

Cid squared her shoulders. "I suppose she told you this and you bought it hook, line . . . "

Turning slowly, Tally met Cid's intense gaze. "Yes. That's why we can't find the connection between Melinda and Marsha." She stabbed her finger at Cid. "You're not seeing clearly on this case."

"Bullshit! Why the fuck did she attack you? And why didn't she kill you?"

"She's a calculating predator, Cid. Tonight wasn't her time to kill. She's toying with me. She said she liked our little game of cat-and-mouse. Think about it. Cats play with their prey before devouring it. I'm Marsha's prey. She constantly has her foot on my tail so I can't escape . . . but she's not quite ready to devour me. Not quite ready to let go of the thrill she feels when she scares me. My fear . . . turns her on." Tally touched her ear. The hair on the back of her neck danced. Distaste flashed across her face.

She turned back and faced the mirror. The bruises on her neck were starting to turn a deep bluish purple. The cuts had already scabbed. "On one level, the piece in the paper excited Marsha. She enjoyed the notoriety. On another level, in that terrible, screwed-up mind, someone has taken part of her glory by killing Melinda and leaving a rose. Marsha's lost control. In the editorial, Robin pointed the finger at her. That makes her nervous. Edgy. I think Melinda Morgan's murder was a copycat murder. A reproduction, if you will. That doesn't fit in her compulsive, orderly life. She will kill again to regain her control, her territory, but in the meantime she wants the real perpetrator caught, or at least exposed. Marsha Cox is the mistress of her domain, and there is room in it only for her own perversity."

"Justice among thieves?" Cid's laughter was ripe with sarcasm. "Cox is a master manipulator. Careful, Tal, you're suckin' a lot of hot air right now. I don't suppose our enlightened serial killer mentioned anything about Carmen Petricelli?"

Tally looked at Cid for a moment in silence, then dropped her eyes and shook her head. "No." Her expression suddenly reflected doubt.

"You okay?" Cid's voice was filled with compassion.

Tally nodded. She selected a pair of Levis and a yellow turtleneck shirt from the extra clothes she kept in the bathroom closet.

Breaking her silence at last, she said, "My nagging fear is that we're dealing with two killers, each evil and fearless."

Cid stepped into the adjoining conference room and lit a cigarette. Doubt flickered in her eyes. *Two killers?* She shook her head and walked across the room. She looked in the corner closet for some Glenlivet. Instead, she found Johnny Walker and poured herself a stiff drink.

They debriefed while Tally dressed in the other room. When she entered the conference room she looked refreshed. The turtleneck hid the cuts and bruises on her neck.

"Now what?" Cid asked.

Tally turned around so Cid could see that her .38 police special was resting comfortably in the small of her back. "I'm keeping Katie with me. And you?"

"Hampton wants details from your encounter with Cox. I'm meeting him at Rudolpho's for a light dinner. After that, we're heading out to Little Capitan. Got a hunch our friend just might show up tonight."

"Marsha's paranoid, Cid. Please be careful. You've discovered her hiding place; she has nowhere to go now, and nothing to lose."

◻ ◻ ◻

Susanna Farrell had lived in Goose Creek all of her life, Tally learned, as she slowly drew information from the South Carolina resident.

"How long did you know Johnny Lee?"

"He lived with Aunt Ella and me near three years 'fore he got in trouble." Susanna yawned into the phone. It was midnight in South Carolina and Tally's call had awakened her.

"Were the two of you close during that time?"

"Yes. He was like kin. Treated me real good till he got 'fatuated. Then he was like a 'coon huntin' for food. Sniffin' in my business. Never takin' his eyes off me."

Tally shifted in the comfortable cordovan leather chair that had once belonged to her father. "Tell me what happened."

"I don't mean Johnny no harm, but I sure was glad when they took him away. He went plumb crazy. If another boy so much as looked at me, he was swingin' those fists of his. It was downright embarrassin'. First I thought he was protectin' me like a little brother. Uh-uh, I was wrong. He took to lookin' at me, you know, like he was undressin' me with his eyes. I told Aunt Ella—'course he never acted that way 'round her."

"How long was this going on?" Tally asked.

"'Bout a year."

"Then what happened?"

"Came in my room that night. Right after I turned the lights out. Aunt Ella was at a church social. Johnny mumbled somethin' 'bout me bein' his. Next thing I knew he was on top of me kissin' me. Thought it was funny at first. Guess I even enjoyed it a bit. But I got scared when he pulled back the covers. That's when I could feel him. His manly part. I screamed. Even scratched his face."

Deep within her, Tally felt a chill.

"I couldn't stop him," Susanna Farrell continued. "He was so strong."

Her voice was hollow now. "When he was done, he said he was sorry. I was cryin'. He kept rubbin' my face, tryin' to make me feel better, I guess. I just wanted him away from me. Started screamin'. He told me to be quiet. You hafta understand," Susanna pleaded, "I didn't even know I was hollerin'. That's when he started hittin' me. I guess I musta kept hollerin', then he put his big hands around my neck and squeezed. Don't 'member nothin' after that till I woke up in the hospital."

Pain crossed Tally's face as she remembered the arm on her own throat. "What stopped him?"

"Aunt Ella came home." Susanna's voice was bitter but calm. "Hit him 'longside the head with a broom. Called the police."

Tally clenched her fists.

"I loved Johnny. Sisterly, mind you. Used to even bake his favorite cookies for him. He hurt me real bad. Near broke my heart."

"Why were the charges dropped?" Tally asked.

Susanna's next words had a familiar ring. "I guess I somehow felt responsible."

14

Tuesday, July 7
10:03 P.M.

The top four floors of San Francisco General were hidden by thick fog, giving the brick building a short, squatty look. Three teenagers had just arrived by ambulance at the emergency entrance. All three were victims of gunshot wounds from a gang-related incident. Two police cruisers were parked at odd angles around the ambulance, their red and blue lights still flashing.

Katie unbuckled her seat belt. "I thought we'd be seeing Harry at the lab."

Slowly, Tally answered, "First, I need to do something else. I called him. He said he'd wait for us."

Obviously preoccupied, Tally checked the rearview mirror before she opened her door.

Although it was still warm outside, the fog made the air damp. Katie shivered, hugging her navy fleece jacket more closely to her body. "You're sure I can't just be waitin' in the car?"

Tally shook her head vigorously. "No. It's not safe." She turned and looked around. "There's a waiting room just across from emergency. You can sit there or come downstairs with me."

"Lovely choice," Katie chided. Her face glowed red and blue from the flashing lights as they walked past the patrol cars.

A dispatcher's voice echoed from inside the empty vehicle. "Three Henry seven report."

Katie moved closer, her feet nearly tangling with Tally's. "I'll stay with you."

□ □ □

Johnny Lee was sitting on a stool in the corner of the lab. His back rested against the wall. His white lab coat was carelessly tossed on the work bench. He was drinking from a carton of Foremost milk. A stack of chocolate-chip cookies wrapped in torn cellophane sat in front of him.

Katie lingered by the door; Tally approached Johnny, then paused.

"Good evening, Johnny," she said with cold, calm clarity.

He stared at her, setting his half-eaten cookie in front of him. "Ma'am." He looked tired. For a second Tally thought she caught a look of fear in his eyes.

Tally sat down on a nearby stool. Her eyes swept the room. "You've cleaned up since I was here last."

"Yes, ma'am." He brushed his hand through his white hair and reached jerkily for his lab coat.

Pointing at the cellophane-wrapped cookies, she asked, "Melinda used to bake you cookies, didn't she? Chocolate chip?"

He nodded, his eyes finally meeting hers suspiciously. Tiny white bristles dotted his cheeks: Johnny Lee hadn't shaved, and it made him look older than twenty-three.

Tally lowered her voice. "Susanna Farrell baked you chocolate-chip cookies too, right?"

A spasm of panic crossed his face. His stomach heaved. He glanced at Katie, who still stood by the door, and then at Tally. "Susanna's a liar. She's workin' with a brick shy of a full load." He sat up straighter, his body rigid.

"Really?" Tally smiled sardonically. "Then Susanna didn't bake you cookies?"

Johnny fidgeted with a button on his lab coat. "Yes, ma'am, she baked cookies. Baked cookies for me. But she's still a damn liar."

Tally stood; she could see Johnny Lee's anger building. She turned to look at Katie as if to downplay her next words. Her voice was very soft. "Why is she a liar, Johnny?"

His eyes were wild. "Look here," he said shakily, "I got work to do."

Tally spun back toward Johnny. "You raped Susanna, Johnny, and then you tried to kill her. She was your family. She loved you like a brother."

Her eyes narrowed. She took a step closer. "Is that how you treat family? Is that how you treated Melinda Morgan?"

The corner of Johnny's mouth twitched. Tears welled up in his eyes. "I never hurt Melinda none. I loved her."

"Just like you loved Susanna?"

"No!"

Katie jumped, her back pressed against the door. Her hands kneaded her lips.

"I loved Melinda like she was my mama." His voice shook so badly he could barely talk. "I wouldn't hurt her none."

His red-rimmed eyes were pleading now. "She knew 'bout Susanna. It made her plenty mad. She sent me to a clinic down on Folsom Street. I still go. We talk 'bout rape. I ain't touched a woman . . . not in a bad way since Susanna. Never will. I promised Melinda, and I ain't about to break my word."

Tally was very still. "What's the name of the clinic?"

Johnny used the sleeve of his lab coat to wipe his face. He stared at her for a long time. "Clinic's name is Control. Man by the name of James Myers runs the meetins. You check with him."

Tally took another step forward. "I intend to notify the local police of your rape and attempted murder of Susanna Farrell."

Johnny jumped to his feet. "I was just a kid."

"Acting like a selfish man out of control!"

Johnny Lee was powerfully built, with wide shoulders, though he stood only five feet six inches tall. It annoyed him and added to his mounting frustration that he had to look up when he addressed Tally. "What d'you all want from me?"

Tally sat back down. "The truth."

"I done told you all I know."

Tally shrugged. "Then I'll be on my way."

She paused for effect. "I assume you realize that by the time the police and the media have finished questioning you, your employer and your friends will know you're a rapist and a suspect in a murder investigation?"

Johnny's shoulders slumped. His eyes flashed toward Katie and the door, but he couldn't escape Tally's scrutiny.

Tally spoke carefully now. She had to pull him in, get him to trust her.

"I'll tell you something, Johnny. Despite the events in your past, you do have one redeeming attribute. You're a loyal friend. You've stuck by Dr. Toliver even at the risk of your own exposure. I wonder if she'd do the same for you? You know her best. Would she risk her career, her friends, maybe even her future for you?"

Burying his head in his hands, he moaned. "I don't know much more. Just that the damn scalpel is missin' and she told me not to say nothin'."

Tally reached out and touched his shoulder. "Tell me about it," she said softly.

"Christmas, couple of years ago, me and the rest of the staff got the doc a scalpel. You know, one of them fancy jobs: engraved with her name and a snap-in blade." He looked up at Tally, his eyes heavy with sadness. "It's been missin' since the night Melinda died. Doc knew it was gone 'fore she left work that night. Told me not to say nothin'."

"What do you think happened to it?"

His words were flat. "Don't know. She always carried it with her in a little case. It was real special."

Johnny looked up, eyes questioning. "Hell, the police found the murder weapon. 'Sides, Becky just wouldn't kill Melinda."

He looked at Tally again, hoping she could tell him Rebecca Toliver wasn't guilty of Melinda's murder.

"When did you know the scalpel was missing?" Tally asked.

Johnny spread his hands. "Don't know exactly. Eleven thirty, maybe even midnight. I was havin' trouble. Most of the time we use the slicin' machine. Sometimes we use our scalpels. Depends what we're cuttin'. I asked for help. She was still sad. Wasn't saying much. She needed a scalpel and asked for mine. That's when I knew hers was missin'. When I asked 'bout it she got mad. She got a disposable out of the drawer."

"Couldn't the scalpel have been missing for days?" Katie asked suddenly.

Johnny's eyes flicked to the door and then back to Tally. "Is she police?"

"She's my business partner at the Phoenix Detective Agency: Katie O'Neil."

Johnny blinked. "I seen it the same night Melinda died. The night before, Becky had me stick it in the autoclave. I gave it back to her when our shift began the next night. The night Melinda was murdered. Watched her put it in the case."

"And the case was always with her?"

"No, ma'am. She usually left it in the top drawer of her desk when she went home. Otherwise it was in her pocket."

Tally turned on him abruptly. "Have you ever been arrested for peeping?"

The charge startled Johnny. "No, ma'am."

"How about eavesdropping?" Her tone held contempt. "Sitting outside of Melinda and Rebecca's bedroom door at night may not be a prosecutable offense, Johnny, but it's certainly sick."

Johnny sat paralyzed, his eyes darting, as if looking for a way out. "It's not what you're thinkin'. I just had to be there." His voice was tight, filled with hatred. "You'll never understand. I had to protect her."

"Who?"

"Melinda," he answered with anguish. "I didn't want her hurt none. Becky used to hit her with her hand, sometimes her cane. Weren't like Melinda did somethin' wrong; Becky'd just get upset. She didn't mean to hurt her none. Melinda said it was cuz Becky worked too hard. When it was over I'd always hear Becky cry . . . say she was sorry."

"How often did this happen?" Tally asked with disgust.

"Never when I first moved in, then maybe, every coupla months," Johnny murmured in a strained voice. "Then all the time."

Looking into Johnny's eyes, Tally read resentment.

He folded his hands and then began to weep. "I loved her, and Becky too." He looked frightened. "I only tried to help . . . that's all."

Tally was too honest with herself to deny her intense dislike of Johnny Lee, but at the same time she felt sorry for him. Melinda Morgan and Rebecca Toliver had probably been the only stable influence in his life, and in the end, even they had betrayed him.

In the silent pink hall, just outside the pathology lab, Tally took Katie's hand in hers. In her mind, the picture of Rebecca Toliver beating Melinda Morgan ran like an unedited piece of bad film.

"I'm sorry," Tally began quietly. "I'm sorry for taking you for granted. Please forgive me."

Katie looked at her, surprised by the sudden apology. "There's been damage," she said softly, "and hurt, but I never saw you as unflawed, Tally McGinnis. If you believe we can still make our love work, then we can. Because I still love you far too much not to try."

Tally held her close. "I'm not afraid of commitment," she said, "only of losing you because of my own selfish behavior."

Katie felt the pressure of Tally's body against hers. She knew she would love Tally more than she had ever been loved before. And, in time, their commitment to each other would be unbreakable.

Tally suddenly quickened her pace and Katie was having a hard time keeping up.

"Lockdown at the jail is at eleven." Tally checked her watch. "We've got to hurry."

The county jail was a straight shot up Potrero and a few blocks down Bryant.

As they drove, Katie rang up Rita Cruz and passed the cellular phone to Tally.

Tally didn't mince words. "I need your help. I'm en route to the Hall of Justice now. I must speak to Rebecca Toliver. It'll only take ten minutes."

Rita hesitated. "Tal, there's no visitation at night."

"The phone. Can I talk to her on the phone? Five minutes max." Her voice was desperate.

The attorney sighed. "I trust you're not going to tell me what this is all about?" She waited for a second; when there was no reply she continued. "I've got sources. I'll try. Give me fifteen minutes. What number?"

Tally parked the BMW in back of the Hall of Justice and again picked up the phone. She got Alberta Rogers' number from information. On the fifth ring the older woman picked up.

"This is Tally McGinnis, Ms. Rogers. Forgive me for calling so late."

"Why, yes, dear, it's no imposition at all. I was just reading. Obviously you wouldn't have called unless it was important. How can I help you?"

"Just one question, and I'm afraid it's not an easy one to answer. Was Dr. Toliver mistreating Melinda . . . abusing her?"

For a moment Alberta Rogers was quiet. "My dear, I have dedicated my life to Rebecca. If I answer that question it will all have been for naught. I am too old and too close to death to face life's cruel realities. I am sorry."

"Well?" Katie asked as she hung up the phone for Tally.

A sense of sadness crept over Tally. "This time I wish Johnny Lee had lied."

"That poor woman," Katie said at length. "How sad Melinda's life must have been. Is it possible the doctor really killed her?"

Katie's gaze was as bleak as her own thoughts. The same doubt had haunted her. "I don't know," Tally finally answered.

Ten minutes later the phone rang.

"This is Dr. Toliver."

Tally gave the thumbs-up sign to let Katie know Rita Cruz had worked her magic.

"Dr. Toliver, this is Tally McGinnis. Sorry to disturb you so late." She wanted to add, *Hope I didn't interrupt anything,* but thought better of it.

"What is it you want from me?" the doctor questioned, her voice edgy. Rebecca Toliver was in unfamiliar territory. She didn't know what to say or, for that matter, how to act. For more than a month she had hidden in her cell as much as possible. She avoided exercising in the yard, except when the guards ordered her to do so, and fervently avoided contact with the other prisoners. When the guard came to take her to the phone she had been taunted and sworn at. She felt like a piece of meat on a conveyor belt as she was led from her cell. The phone call, a special privilege, could only increase her odds of being hurt. She was frightened.

"Your personally engraved scalpel, Doctor—where is it?"

"What?" The question had caught the doctor off guard. Foolishly, she lied to buy time. "I don't know what you're talking about."

"Was your scalpel the real murder weapon?" How Tally wished she were face-to-face with Rebecca Toliver. She wished Alberta Rogers was at her side. The old woman would have known if the doctor was lying.

The doctor's face turned to stone. "Don't be absurd." She looked around nervously. "There's a guard here."

"Of course there is," Tally snapped, "and in a few weeks there will be a whole courtroom full of people listening to you answer the same question."

"I told you I had nothing to do with Melinda's murder." She lowered her voice. "I loved her."

"Where's your scalpel?"

Her chin dropped to her chest. "At the hospital," she whispered. "Pediatric floor."

"Be specific," Tally pushed.

The doctor turned her back to the guard, cupping her hand over the phone. "I'll lose my license to practice," she wailed.

"Your choice, Doctor. Tell me now or I call the police when we hang up."

"I threw it on top of the drug cabinet. The blade is broken. I was trying to pry the cabinet door open to get a bottle out when I heard someone coming down the hall. I panicked. The blade snapped. Melinda had only enough morphine to get her through the night. I needed drugs so I could wean her off of them slowly."

"What about Dr. Spencer Jewell?"

Rebecca's voice took on a new determination. "I couldn't call him."

"Why?"

"He's slime."

"Oh," Tally said, trying to keep the judgment out of her voice. "I guess it's better to break into a drug cabinet in a pediatric oncology ward?"

Rebecca's mouth was dry. "Melinda owed Jewell fifty thousand dollars."

Tally shook her head. "The picture is clearer now. Why did you throw the scalpel on top of the cabinet?"

"I said I panicked. Later, when I went back to get it, I realized the cabinet was too high. I couldn't very well bring a step stool in, could I? I'd already made up one excuse for being on the floor in the first place. I didn't need someone snooping around. I threw away the case that I normally stored the scalpel in and figured I'd report it stolen the next day. What difference does it make anyway?"

"It could be the real murder weapon."

"How many times do I have to tell you I didn't have anything to do with Melinda's murder?" Her voice was filled with rage.

The prison guard was staring openly at her. "I'll see to it that not one penny of your fee is paid by Rita Cruz."

At that, Tally laughed. "I don't think so, Doctor. Rita is a consummate professional. She is both ethical and honest."

Tally looked at Katie, as if to gain strength. Her tone was casual and off the cuff, which drove home her point all the more. "You may or may not be a murderer. I don't know for sure yet. But tell me, Doctor, did Melinda begin to use drugs because of a back injury, or to soften the hurt and humiliation of living with an abuser?"

The phone went dead.

15

Tuesday, July 7
11:15 P.M.

The double-door entry to the back of the pathology lab opened with electronic precision. A stretcher was rapidly wheeled out through the door, collapsed, and shoved into the back of the white medical examiner's utility vehicle. Partially obscured by dark shadows and dense fog, a figure entered the van. A few seconds later, glaring headlights caused both Tally and Katie to shield their eyes as they walked across the parking lot. Tires squealed as the van raced out of the fenced area.

Light from the open door served as their beacon. They quickly scurried up the stairs.

The security guard looked surprised when they walked into the hall. Recognizing the guard, Tally called out, "Relax, Smokey, Harry's expecting us."

The old man answered with a wave of his hand.

Chief Medical Examiner Harry Sinclaire was not in the autopsy theater. The large room was dark except for a single light that glowed over the refrigeration unit that served as the temporary home for the dead. Bodies were brought in at all hours of the day and night. For that reason, the light was never turned off.

Harry's desk was stacked with case files, autopsy reports awaiting his final signature, and, next to his computer, printouts containing budgetary outlines and supply costs. A small framed picture, yellow with age, showed a woman Harry had long ago known and loved. She had died in an automobile accident when he was still in college. On the opposite side of the desk stood a larger, oak-framed picture of Tally, Patrick, and Victoria McGinnis that had been taken when Tally graduated from high school.

Harry's back was to the door and his fingers moved rapidly across the keyboard of his computer. His white lab coat was draped across the back of his chair. He glanced around. "If I didn't know better, I'd think you were a spy for the city, intent on getting every last drop of energy from this tired, overworked body. It's after eleven o'clock." He smiled as he swiveled his chair around to face them.

"Katie, lass, what a sight for very tired eyes." He reached out and took her hand in his, squeezing it warmly.

She bent down and kissed his bushy, bearded cheek. "Aye, it's good to see you, too." Her face was flushed with pleasure.

"I'm sorry we're so—"

Harry cut Tally off. "Got a call from Grayson Chandler late this afternoon. Told me about your visit. He wanted me to send him pictures from both the Morgan and Petricelli cases."

Tally noticed that tonight Harry's face had the carefully schooled hardness of a medical expert working violent, repugnant cases. "Your visit bothered me last night." He pointed at his head. "It got the tumblers rolling. Fifteen minutes after you left, Petricelli's body was wheeled into autopsy. You know much about the murder?"

Tally shook her head. "I know Carmen was murdered, and that the M.O. was very similar to the Dorset homicide, right down to a red rose being left at the scene." Both women sat down in matching black leather chairs.

Harry loosened his gaudy yellow-and-orange tie and unfastened the top button of his white shirt. "Ahh, should have done that hours ago."

He gave Tally a measured look. "At first glance the case was consistent with the Dorset murder: body abused, arterial tube in the femoral artery."

"At first glance?" Tally zeroed in.

Harry's fingers formed a tent. "Rage," he finally said. "Grayson looks into the psyche and tags the killer with the label 'sociopath.' I look at the savageness of his or her work. A pattern develops. Maybe there's a certain way of breaking bones, cutting flesh. Cox likes to bleed her victims to death. Although the actual elapsed time period is relatively short, she must enjoy watching life ooze from her victims. I studied the pictures of Melinda Morgan and I agree with Grayson that the precision and compulsive neatness that Cox displayed in the previous killing is consistent with this case. But . . . for whatever reason . . . she is showing no rage or savagery this time. This is a red flag. The Petricelli case is the same. I reviewed everything. All my notes, pictures—I even viewed Petricelli's body again before the funeral home picked it up. The cruelty is missing."

Katie whimpered. It was now clearer than ever why she enjoyed managing the office and leaving the footwork to Cid and Tally.

"Are you all right?" Tally asked, concern in her voice.

"Aye," she winked, "but you can bloody well believe I'll be staying at the office from now on."

Tally looked back at Harry, her green eyes not as bright as when she first arrived. "I don't understand," she said, pushing her bangs back with a frustrated gesture. "Carmen Petricelli was beat up and bled to death. I certainly see that as cruel."

Harry reached for a pack of Marlboros. "I need a smoke. Mind?"

"Yes," Katie answered.

Harry nodded, pushing the cigarettes aside. "You've made an assumption. Petricelli was not bled to death. Someone tried, but it was a feeble attempt. The arterial tube was put in upside down. The tube caused a small hemorrhage, but the cause of death was strangulation. As for being beat up, there was damage, but no gross violence. Not like when Cox killed the Dorset woman."

Tally shifted forward in her seat and pressed her fingertips against Harry's desk; her eyes were wide. "Copycat," she whispered.

Harry nodded. "That would be my assessment. And after Grayson reviewed the pictures and other data I sent him, he too agrees that the crime looks like the work of a copycat murderer."

"And Melinda Morgan?"

"Same killer. I think I told you yesterday that the laser picked up a few fibers on the body. Common cotton and wool. Same wool fibers were found on Petricelli's body. Brown in color."

Tally slapped her hands together. "I knew it!" She looked at Katie. "That means Dr. Toliver is innocent . . . at least of killing Melinda. And if it's not Marsha Cox, who is it? Could it be a drug killing?"

Harry stood and stretched. "Certainly someone who wanted the police to believe it was Cox. Figure out where the perp got his or her info, and you'll find the killer."

Tally looked at Katie as if to confirm what she was saying. "If that's the guideline, it could have been anybody. Cox's escapades have been well trumpeted by the media."

Harry yawned. "Well, ladies, you can theorize all you want. I'm going home to bed."

"Wait, just two more questions. Why were the samples of Marsha Cox's blood missing from this lab?"

He was silent. Tally knew how proud Harry was of his department. Misplaced evidence was a slap in his face. A mark against his management skills and his staff's competence.

"Don't know, but it's under active investigation." Harry's knuckles were white as he tightly clenched his hand into a fist. "The section chief, Carol Vincovich, was off today. Out of town. She holds the answers. I expect to hear from her before I leave, or at home tonight."

Tally fished in her pants pocket and retrieved the small scrap of paper she had found at Rebecca Toliver's house. "Does this mean anything to you?"

Harry took the paper. "Let's have a look under the scope."

They walked down the hall. Harry slipped his master key into the lock and flicked on the lights.

"Toxicology," he said.

The countertops were cluttered with bottles of every shape imaginable. Some contained liquids, others pills in various shapes and colors. Books lined the walls. Katie noticed one volume that stood out from the others. It had black binding printed with bold white letters that simply read, "CYANIDE."

Harry moved to one of several microscopes lined up on the counter and turned on a small light. He viewed the paper carefully. "Some type of waxy coating on the inside, of the kind used to protect dated material. Could be candy, although I doubt it. I don't see any residue to suggest chocolate or any other sticky material. Is this important?" He looked up from the scope.

Tally shrugged. "I found it in the closet just down the hall from Melinda Morgan's bedroom. It could have been dropped by anyone. Could have been dropped by the murderer. Dr. Toliver mentioned she smelled peppermint the night Melinda was killed. If you give that a good sniff you'll smell peppermint, too."

"Police must have overlooked this. I'll have some tests run on it first thing in the morning. Give me a call about nine o'clock."

Tally frowned. "What if the murderer is getting ready to strike again? After all, there was a major editorial in this afternoon's paper about Marsha Cox. It inflamed Marsha, so I would imagine it would do the same to the copycat." Tally pulled back the collar of her turtleneck, revealing her bruised neck.

Harry inhaled sharply.

"Please do that test now."

The Chief Medical Examiner considered for a moment, his hands stroking his beard. "It's not my field, and the Phoenix Detective Agency's needs aren't part of my budget." He glanced at Tally's neck. "Let me see who's here. But next time," he said, not blinking an eye, "you take this sort of thing to an independent lab." He took the fragment of paper and disappeared down another hallway.

Tally turned the lights off and closed the door to toxicology. She paced the worn floor tile while Katie went to the restroom.

Harry returned five minutes later. His mood had improved. "You know," he said, wiping his forehead with his handkerchief, "Marsha Cox isn't the only compulsive person involved in this case." He gave Tally's hand a gentle squeeze. "We should know something in about thirty minutes."

Katie was discussing the IRA with Harry when Tally slipped out to use the pay phone. Cid, who was staked out at Little Capitan Park, answered her car phone after one ring.

Tally quickly updated Cid on Harry's findings.

"So you were right after all: it was another killer," Cid conceded.

Tally laughed. "You were right about one thing: Marsha Cox is still in the area." She touched her neck.

"Well she's not out here. At least not yet." Cid sounded grumpy.

"Hampton with you?"

"No. He's got a small stakeout team down below. They're pulling an all-nighter. I'm sitting peacefully on top of the mountain, counting stars. No fog up here."

"Sounds romantic. Too bad you're alone," she teased.

"Gotta be someone out there who appreciates cellulite and love handles. I'll find her," Cid chuckled.

"How long do you plan to stay?"

Cid checked her watch. "Another hour. Give me a call if anything breaks. And Tal, be careful."

❏ ❏ ❏

Bertrum Dietrick was a skinny, bespectacled know-it-all most of the other technicians couldn't stand to be around. Harry had assigned him to the night shift because it was solitary duty. His work was flawless and he was willing to share his knowledge with anyone who could tolerate his nasal, high-pitched voice.

"More tests are indicated for me to determine evidentiary findings." Bertrum adjusted the thick, black-framed glasses on his narrow nose. "I can decisively state, however, that the substance bound within this wrapper contained mineral oil, starch, and calcium."

"Your best guess?" Harry asked impatiently.

Bertrum gave him a long, expressionless look. "I haven't one, and the computer I need is down until morning."

16

Wednesday, July 8
1:02 A.M.

"Copycat?" Katie questioned. "Wouldn't it be very difficult to copy Marcia Cox's unique M.O.?"

Tally turned the key in the BMW's ignition. "Definitely difficult." She sighed. "I believe that poor Carmen Petricelli was murdered for convenience."

Katie turned sideways, draped her arm across the back of the seat, and rested her fingers on Tally's shoulder. "I don't understand." Her brow was furrowed.

Braking for a stoplight, Tally looked over at Katie thoughtfully. "When Cathy Dorset was murdered, only a few people were actually involved in the case. The Dorset family was on the fringe, but was never really involved. That leaves the police, you, Cid, myself, and Carmen Petricelli. Carmen was an easy target. She could be linked to the Cox family and to Marsha. It was masterful planning. The odd thing is, her name was never mentioned in the newspaper. Only three of us knew she was helping me."

The silence spun out. In the fog, headlights looked like big-eyed monsters crawling up the hills.

Tally felt incredibly sad. While trying to protect Katie, she had unfortunately involved her in a dangerous murder investigation. The mistake, she realized, too late, of a loving heart.

When the stoplight turned green, Tally turned left and abruptly right into a parking lot. The inside of the car was instantly filled with crimson neon light from a sign that flashed, "OPEN 24 HOURS."

"What are we doing at Payless Drugs?" Katie asked, surprised by Tally's sudden departure from the normal route home.

"Mineral oil, starch, and calcium. We're looking for a label."

The pharmacist behind the counter was not much help. He pointed to the vitamins. "I'd start there; it's as good a place as any."

Tally and Katie read label after label until their eyes blurred and ingredients blended together. Tally felt as if she was racing against the clock, drawn unwillingly into the scheme of some insidious killer whose sole goal was to mislead and confuse her.

The two women separated, each taking an aisle and searching the shelves with reduced enthusiasm. At 3:15 Tally found Katie sitting on the floor, boxes of candy strewn around her. She held up three candy bars. "Remind me never to be eatin' candy again," she instructed with a frown. "Artificial flavors, malic acid, egg albumen, carnauba wax . . . bloody hell, sounds like a mixture toxicology ought to be checkin'."

Tally smiled wearily. "Let's go. We could look for the next three days and not find what we need."

"We can't be givin' up," Katie protested.

"We're not." Tally palmed a Butterfinger. "We'll just hit it from another angle."

"Surely," Katie protested, pointing at Tally's hand, "you're not about to eat that?"

Tally made a feeble attempt to smile. "My one indulgence."

They stopped at the checkout to pay for the candy bar. Just in front of them a uniformed police officer was purchasing a pack of cigarettes. The rest of the store was quiet, as were the streets outside. Most sane people were asleep this time of the night.

Tally picked up a box of wintergreen Tic Tacs, glanced at the ingredients, and tossed them on the counter with her candy bar.

Her eyes drifted across the sales rack. *TV Guide, Star,* the *Enquirer,* Dentyne, Juicy Fruit, Rolaids.

"Holy shit," she breathed, her heart banging against her ribs. She looked at the uniformed officer standing in front of her, feeling a sense of betrayal as she reached for a blue-and-white-wrapped package of Tums. Slowly she rolled the package in her hand. "Active ingredients: Calcium, mineral oil, starch, talc, sodium."

Placing her thumb over the letters TU, her hands trembled. She knew the remaining letters, MS, would match the small fragment of paper she had left with Harry.

Katie knew what Tally was thinking. Together they read the front of the small cylindrical package: *Peppermint.* TUMS *Regular Strength.*

□ □ □

Tally sped down Market Street, hitting each light as it systematically turned green, as if the hands of justice were guiding the controls.

She glanced at Katie. "Call Cid."

The phone rang ten times. "No answer. I'll try her car phone." Several seconds passed. The car was deathly quiet.

"No answer," Katie reported again, her voice tinged with alarm.

"Damn." Tally banged her fist on the steering wheel and then pushed her hand through her hair, as if willing her brain to think.

"Call information; get the number for Jack Bartlett. He works Homicide with Barney Hampton. When you get him on the line I'll talk to him."

Tally pulled into one of many empty metered spaces along Market Street. "Jack, it's Tally McGinnis."

Inspector Jack Bartlett was a big-bellied, black-haired man who had sharp features, a penchant for cigars, and a bellowing voice. He had been disciplined many times in his twenty-eight-year career with the San Francisco Police Department and reduced in rank twice for drinking on the job. Since he had joined AA, however, his record was spotless.

"McGinnis, it's fucking three thirty in the morning. What the hell do you want?"

"About the Morgan and Petricelli murders. You know the cases?" Tally heard a lighter click twice and knew the inspector had lit a cigar.

"Yeah. They're Hampton's cases. Call him."

"Can't," Tally said grimly. "I think he's dirty."

"What the fuck? You drunk?"

"Hardly. Evidence is circumstantial at this point. But I believe the unidentified blood found at the Morgan crime scene will nail Barney. He also should have a newly healed scratch or a fresh scar somewhere. Since he was probably wearing a jacket, I'd check his hands and arms. Brown wool fibers were found at both scenes. Get Hampton's jacket under a microscope and I'll bet my life you find blood from both victims."

"Sounds like horseshit. You expect me to break rank and accuse a fellow officer of murder? If you're not drunk, you should be—at least you'd have an excuse. Shit, the woman's damn earlobes were missing. Barney's no weirdo."

"Jack, Cid's missing. At least I think she is. She was out at Little Capitan with Hampton. Different cars, different locations. I can't raise her at home or on her car phone."

"You *think* Barney's a murderer. You *think* Cid's missing." He laughed and then coughed, the dry hack of a heavy smoker. "Just whatta you want me to do, Tally?"

"Trust me. I was a good cop when I was on the force, and you know it. My guts are screaming at me. Only three people were privy to the fact that Carmen Petricelli was helping me nail Marsha Cox. Myself, Cid, and Barney. He's dirty, Jack."

"Where are you?" he asked, his voice suddenly quiet.

"On my way to Little Capitan."

"I'll meet you at the entrance in twenty minutes. And, McGinnis, if this turns out to be bullshit, I'll burn your P.I. license in front of every cop on the force."

17

Wednesday, July 8
3:57 a.m.

All Tally's pent-up frustrations of the past two days coalesced in the next few minutes. Inspector Jack Bartlett's police-issue, white Chevy Caprice skidded on gravel as it came to a stop next to Tally's BMW. Dressed in wrinkled gray slacks and a navy blue windbreaker with the word "POLICE" stenciled on the back, he looked as if he had slept in his clothes.

"McGinnis," he barked, as he got out of the car and shone his flashlight on the BMW. "What's the location of the stakeout team?"

His thick cigar wobbled in his mouth as he spoke, the amber end glowing in the semidarkness.

Tally shrugged. It was apparent the inspector had not called the station, which meant he was still protecting Barney.

"I'm not sure, but it's not a large area." She looked around. "No backup?"

Inspector Bartlett leaned close to the window and cigar smoke instantly filled the car. He seemed to be on a mental seesaw as he studied Tally's face in the dim light. Barney Hampton was his former partner. The bond was closer than that between brothers.

"Got the stakeout team for backup," he finally said with effort. The atmosphere was tense. "Heard from Cid?"

Tally shook her head. "We've continued to try." She glanced at Katie with a worried look, then turned back to Bartlett. "No answer on either phone. Last time I talked with her she was here, at the summit."

They both looked in the direction Tally was pointing, but the fog was too thick to see beyond the trees that stood only a few feet ahead.

Jack Bartlett hitched up his pants. His belt rode high in the back and dipped low in front to buckle beneath his protruding belly. "Let's go."

"To the summit?" Tally asked, meeting Jack's eyes.

Inspector Bartlett was quiet for a moment as he looked at her. "No," he said finally. "Cameron's probably with Barney. She may be retired, but she's cop through and through. She needs to be where the action is. Never paid any attention to regs when she was on the force, doubt she'd start now."

The comment only increased Tally's worry. Without responding, she opened the car door.

The telephone beeped, breaking the silence of the night. Tally and Katie jumped.

Katie was quiet for a moment, phone pressed to her ear. Then she passed the receiver to Tally. "It's Harry," she said, the disappointment in her voice undeniable.

Tally glanced at her watch. "Don't you ever sleep?" she said, surprised by the sudden call.

"Only the dead rest." Harry's words were clipped. "Carol Vincovich got back in town late this afternoon, called me about fifteen minutes ago. Thought you might find this interesting. She's been tracking Marsha Cox's missing blood sample half the night. Six months ago Vincovich's lab assistant, Gab

Caplan, had a brother who was arrested for armed robbery, a liquor store. Gab just happens to play poker with Barney Hampton and three other guys every Thursday night. Get the picture? They're poker buddies.

"Well, a couple of days after the arrest, Gab runs into Barney Hampton and asks him if there's anything he could do to get the robbery charges reduced for the brother. A week later, the owner of the liquor store that was held up suddenly gets a bad case of amnesia and can't identify Gab Caplan's brother. Charges were dropped.

"There's more. About a month ago Barney goes to Caplan and asks him to lose the Cox blood sample. Gab refuses and Barney reminds him about his brother. Insinuates the liquor store owner might still be able to identify him. Tells Caplan he owes him, big time."

Harry paused, his voice weary and disgusted. "Barney threatens Caplan that his body would be sporting a toe tag if he doesn't cooperate and keep his mouth shut."

There was a nauseating simplicity in the last sentence that sent shivers up Tally's spine. Jack Bartlett, his head close to Tally's, pulled away from the phone and shook his head. "Bullshit," he said under his breath. "Caplan's protecting his own ass."

Tally held the phone tightly. "But, Harry, how did Vincovich determine that Caplan was responsible for removing Cox's blood sample?"

"Vincovich did a little detective work of her own and discovered that Caplan was the last person to handle Cox's blood sample. She threatened him with charges of tampering with evidence in an active murder investigation, and Caplan began to sing." Harry took a deep breath. "This whole business makes me sick. Hampton's one of us, for Christ's sake. Nail him, Tal! But please be careful."

Jack Bartlett seemed almost grateful that the call was completed and motioned for Tally to hurry up.

"Keep the car door locked," Tally instructed, handing the phone back to Katie. And then she reached behind her and brought her .38 into view. "Don't hesitate to use this if you have to," she said, sliding the gun across the seat before getting out of the car.

Jack Bartlett's flashlight was of little help in the fog. Brittle underbrush snapped as they pushed through the darkness. "How far did you say this was?"

"The base of the mountain should be about a hundred yards ahead."

They walked on, stumbling over rocks and sawed-off tree stumps.

"Christ," the inspector mumbled, "this is like 'Nam. Can't see where the hell you're going or what the hell is waiting for you." Finally he clicked the light off and slipped it in his jacket pocket. Transferring his 9mm to his free hand, he mopped his face with his handkerchief.

Suddenly, the immense glare from a Kel light shone in their faces. Tally nearly dropped to her knees from the shock.

"Shit," the inspector yelled. "Turn that damn thing down."

"Bartlett? That you?"

Barney Hampton lumbered out from the swirling shadows. Surprise tinged his face as he moved into the light.

A uniformed officer appeared behind Tally and Inspector Bartlett. Tally watched as he returned his gun to the black leather holster on his waist. The officer crossed his arms, as intrigued as Barney Hampton by the sudden appearance of Jack Bartlett.

"Got a problem, Barn." The quiver in the inspector's voice made Tally suddenly feel sad.

He rolled the cigar in his mouth, stroking it gently and then sucking on it as if it were a straw.

"McGinnis, here, has some ideas about the Morgan and Petricelli murders." He fished in his pocket for his lighter. "Thinks you might know a little more about the cases than you've let on." Jack's face was pained. "I hate to ask these questions, Barn, but you know the drill."

Barney looked positively baffled. "Drill, huh. Well then, while you're bein' so careful to follow procedure, you might keep this in the back of your mind. As far as I'm concerned, McGinnis, here, is still a suspect in the Dorset murder, and it's my belief she'll do anything to deflect the spotlight away from her." He peeled two Tums from a roll. A small piece of paper fluttered in the breeze and dropped to the ground.

No doubt was left in Tally's mind. She wanted to cry.

Placing the Tums in his mouth, Barney stepped back, his face now hidden in the shadows.

The plainclothes officer holding the light slowly turned the beam so that Barney's face was visible again. Tally absentmindedly noticed that his brown tweed jacket didn't match his black slacks. The garment had stretched with age and hung loosely around his shoulders.

"Harry found wool fibers on both victims' bodies," Tally began, her voice weak and a little high-pitched. "It's my guess, Barney, that they came from your jacket. As you know, he found unidentified blood at the scene. I think tests will prove that blood came from you also."

Chuckling, Barney raised his hand to shield his eyes from the glare. "Jack, you buy any of this bullcrap?" His voice was unusually harsh.

Jack Bartlett's lighter flared and big puffs of white smoke encircled his head. "Just take a blood test in the morning, Barn, and it'll all wash."

The furrows on Barney's face seemed to deepen. "Okay. Sure, I could do that."

Tally felt numb. "Wait!" she said, taking a step forward, her tone passionate. "Why lose any time? Melinda Morgan gouged her killer with her finger-nails. Just show us your arms and hands." Her voice rose suddenly. "If there are no fresh scars, hell, Barney, you're home free and I look the fool."

Jack Bartlett pulled his cigar from his mouth and motioned encouragingly to his former partner, his friend, to step forward. But Barney Hampton stood stone still. His eyes were riveted on Tally.

"Carmen was an easy target, wasn't she?" Tally goaded. "She was a kind woman. She probably asked you into her house for coffee. She may even have offered to show you her garden."

Tally continued in measured tones, "But you forgot one important thing, Barney: only three of us knew about Carmen. Cid, myself, and you. Marsha Cox never knew Petricelli had talked to me and supplied incriminating information.

"You brought a rose to the Morgan murder scene, planning carefully to point the finger at Marsha. Then something unexpected happened. You heard the elevator and thought someone was coming. Beyond cutting off the earlobes, you had no chance to further mutilate Melinda's body. You quickly changed your plan and focused the blame on Dr. Toliver. You knew she didn't have an alibi for the time of the murder because you saw her at the house. You were hiding in the closet. How convenient it must have been for you when Dr. Toliver mopped the floor and removed your footprints. You planted the scalpel in Dr. Toliver's trunk and then reaped the praise of your fellow officers when you claimed to have discovered it there. Another notch in your belt to help with your promotion. There was no way you could foresee that Rita Cruz would be hired to defend Dr. Toliver, or that Cid and I would end up on the case. When that happened your panic caused you to change your plans again. You fed Cid just enough information to make her believe Marsha was the murderer. And to protect your neat little scenario, you killed Carmen. Two kind and decent women are dead. Why, Barn? Why?"

Jack Bartlett's face had changed. "Barney?" His tone was not friendly.

All was silent. Barney made no move to defend himself.

Jack turned and signaled to the officer behind him. "Barn, sorry, buddy, I gotta haul you downtown until we can get this mess straightened out."

Suddenly, Barney pulled his gun from the holster and raised it to his head. He looked at Jack and then at Tally.

The patrolman drew his gun and leveled it at Barney's chest.

"Come on, buddy." Jack Bartlett's voice was almost pleading.

"Melinda was the first woman who'd been good to me since my wife died . . . "

"Barney, buddy, don't say another word. You have the right to remain silent. You have the right—"

"I don't care, Jack. It's over for me," Barney ran his free hand through his hair. "Before Melinda moved to Pediatrics, she was my nurse when I was hospitalized. For weeks I used to meet her in the hospital cafeteria for coffee or lunch. Even took her to dinner a few times. She was a good friend and I was so lonely. I loved her. Imagine that—me falling in love, at my age."

Barney bitterly laughed at the memory. "I thought she loved me. Even asked her to marry me. Made a damn fool of myself. Even bought a ring and everything. Oh, she was nice when she told me there was already someone in her life, but I could see the mockery in her eyes." His eyes flickered as he gazed at the night sky. "That was the day before I went to her house. The day before I killed her."

He looked at Tally. "How do you think I felt? A pathetic, middle-aged cop asks a dyke to marry him." Tears were on his cheeks. Now he looked at Jack Bartlett. "Hell, I even bragged to you, Jack, told you I was getting married again. My job, the chief, the commissioner . . . I'd have been the laughingstock. She should have told me, Jack, a long time ago. Damned *dyke bitch*," he spat.

Jack Bartlett drew his gun and pointed it at his friend. "Drop it, Barney, now!"

"Melinda was a good person." Tally's voice shook. "From what I understand, she opened her heart to everyone. She wanted to help people and she wanted to be their friend. She never misled you. She offered you friendship, but that wasn't enough to satisfy you. Two people have died for no reason. Please, Barney, don't add to the count."

The trees, the fog, the gun, and the glare from the lights all blended into a momentary collage. Barney stood still in the middle of it all, looking wooden and lost.

"Cid," Tally managed to say. "Where is she?"

For a second Barney's eyes focused on Tally; the wind ruffled his sandy, graying hair. The patrolman had edged to within a few feet of Barney, and Jack also began walking toward him. "Cid?" Barney cocked his head and smiled. The moment was his and he would say no more.

"Yes, Barney. Cid trusted your instincts—trusted *you*. She believed you were a good cop. She went after Marsha just like you wanted her to. If she's hurt I'll . . . " Tally stopped, struggling to control herself. Her fists were clenched, her eyes filled with anger. "You son of a bitch. You wimpy, gutless son of a bitch."

Suddenly Barney's demeanor changed. His eyes burned with anger. "Did you say 'wimpy', McGinnis? I'll show you . . ."

In a flash, the uniformed officer was on him. Bartlett lunged forward, too, and together they wrestled Barney to the ground. His gun was twisted from his hand. Cuffs were slapped into place and Barney's face was pushed into the soft earth until his breath came in weak gasps.

In a veiled attempt to remain under control, Tally raised her voice. "Jack, the summit! Cid! We've got to get to the summit."

18

Wednesday, July 8
4:41 A.M.

As if on cue, the fog thinned, leaving filtered moonlight as a silvery guide. Katie stood beside the BMW, her face full of hope and fear. A black-and-white skidded to a stop nearby. Tally flung open the back door. Katie jumped in.

The road to the summit of Little Capitan was partly overgrown and was a nightmare of ruts and loose gravel. About halfway up they saw that a gate had been carelessly left open. Tally's stomach felt hollow with the fear of what lay ahead.

At the crest of the thousand-foot mountain the patrolman turned off the headlights, slowed, and pulled off the dirt road. "Stay put until backup arrives," Bartlett commanded. He withdrew his 9mm from the shoulder holster, rolled down the passenger window, and peered outside.

Leaves from the few trees that lined the edge of the granite plateau fluttered in the breeze. Cid's Plymouth Fury sat silently near the rocky precipice. Moonlight pooled on the dull green hood, bounced off the windows, and imitated the stars that were winking in the early-morning sky.

Tally's heart was pounding. She squeezed Katie's hand and was out of the car before Inspector

Bartlett could protest. Her body was a dark sliver as she darted in and out of shadows. Trembling from both cold and fear, she reached for the .38 Katie had just returned to her.

The wind sang a tune reminiscent of old horror movies, its pitch high and eerie. When she reached Cid's car, Tally dropped to her knees. *Please be all right, Cid.* The metal fender was cold to her fingertips. The driver's door hung open. The shadows were too deep for her to see what lay within.

Breathing hard, Tally leaped to her feet, her gun leveled at the interior of the car. Her eyes flashed back and forth, searching frantically for any sign of life. She heard the grinding of pebbles behind her and spun, ready to fire, but it was only Bartlett and Patrolman Jensen quickly moving in.

"You're a fucking idiot, McGinnis," Jack Bartlett whispered harshly, his breath coming in short gasps, his teeth clenched on a cigar.

Tally shifted her weight, her eyes once again riveted on the interior of the car. "Eloquence isn't your strong suit, Jack."

Abruptly, the brilliance from the Kel light flooded the area, and for the three of them, grim reality became a grotesque slow-motion image of a body streaked and spattered with blood.

Red and blue lights from the backup team pulsed in the background as Tally leaned into the Plymouth and touched the carotid artery on the neck of the motionless body. There was no pulse.

Tally's heart was hammering against her ribs. "Oh, God," she moaned.

Jack Bartlett's voice boomed across the plateau. "Get some tape. Cordon the area. Jensen, call Forensics. Goddamnit, get some more light over here."

The victim's upper body was nude. Her pantyhose was still in place, but was torn and cut.

Oddly, one foot, toenails painted red, had slipped free from the hose and seemed to be resting casually on the car seat. Wadded in the victim's mouth was the article from the *Examiner*. The lines "the killings at Little Capitan stand out as examples of sociopathic cruelty and brutality: the work of a twisted, troubled mind" were highlighted in bright yellow ink.

A mortician's arterial tube was skillfully inserted in the victim's right femoral artery and a single, blood-red rose lay on the dashboard.

"Marsha Cox has reclaimed her territory," Tally said tightly, her hands shaking so hard she had trouble holding on to her gun.

"Back off, McGinnis," Bartlett demanded.

Tally's body jerked nervously at the inspector's voice behind her, but she held her ground. She glanced at Jensen, who stood off to one side talking into a hand-held radio.

The car door was bent back at an odd angle, as if someone's body had been hurled against it. The car phone's receiver dangled by its cord from the steering wheel.

Light bars flashing, two more police cars arrived at the summit and disgorged at least a half-dozen men and women in uniforms and plainclothes.

"Ain't Cid," Tally heard the patrolman say into the radio. Stepping forward, careful to preserve the crime scene, the inspector asked Tally almost nonchalantly, "Ever see this dame before?"

"This woman," Tally corrected, her nerves and patience raw, "is Robin Stapleton. She wrote the recent editorial in the *Examiner* about Marsha Cox."

Sirens screamed in the distance, signaling the imminent arrival of more reinforcements. Headlights now fully illuminated the plateau, and Tally's eyes scanned the mountaintop. "Where's Robin's car?"

"Aye. And more important, where's Cid?" Katie's voice was muffled and drained. She shivered as she watched the activities from about ten feet away.

"Not here," Bartlett said, pulling his head from the car and firing up his lighter. "Looks to me like Stapleton was dragged to the car. Blood on the body, but not much in the car. Check out her feet: chips of granite are embedded in her heels."

Tally leaned into the car; Bartlett was correct. Despite her misgivings about the inspector, he was a good cop who took in even the smallest details. "That still doesn't explain where Cid is," Tally said worriedly.

Jack Bartlett directed his Kel light at the ground. Splattered blood, punctuated by a piece of torn pantyhose, ran parallel to the Plymouth. The inspector squatted to examine the evidence more closely, his knees making a popping sound.

Tally leaned over his shoulder. On close scrutiny, she could barely make out two parallel grooves in the gravel. Something clicked in her mind. *Did Marsha surprise Cid, then drag her body? No . . . no. Cid was waiting for Marsha. She never would have been taken by surprise.*

Tally's blood was drumming in her ears now. *It had to be someone Cid trusted. Barney?* Once again her eyes traced the grooves in the gravel. "The trunk! The damned trunk!"

Tally shoved Jensen to one side and reached into the car. "The keys, the fucking keys are missing." She fell to her knees and took a deep breath to center herself. As she slid her hand over the gravelly surface, sharp pieces of granite nipped at her fingertips. Katie and Officer Jensen joined the search.

"Keys," Bartlett yelled, as he headed to the patrol car for a crowbar. "Look on the ground for a set of keys."

From the other side of the car, close to the edge of the cliff, someone yelled, "I've got 'em."

Tally's chest heaved as she gulped air. Before anyone else could move, she raced around the car and grabbed the keys from the uniformed officer. A loud squeal from rusty hinges alerted everyone on the mountaintop that the trunk was opening. All movement stopped.

In the trunk, face down and motionless on the black carpet, was Cid, her gray hair matted with blood. Tally felt for a pulse, then turned her over. Cid was still breathing.

Epilogue

Thursday, July 9
4:45 P.M.

The summer afternoon was hot and still. The leaves on the trees surrounding the red brick hospital building hung limply; white cotton-candy clouds dotted an otherwise blue sky.

"That woman . . . rich bitch . . . society snob," Cid moaned, holding her head with both hands. "If it weren't for her, this never would have happened. Hell, in thirty-some years in law enforcement, I've never been clubbed." She closed her eyes, lowered her head back onto the pillow, and moaned again. When no one responded, she opened one eye and looked around. Her eye fell on Katie. "Maybe you could adjust my pillow just a little," she said coyly.

"Aye, but I'll have you remember, Cid Cameron, you're sufferin' from a concussion and twenty-five stitches, not brain surgery." Katie winked, carefully arranging the pillows.

Tally smiled at the exchange, then looked bewildered. "So, Cid, my mother called you at what time? And why?"

Cid's eyes grew narrow. "Let's see. Barney pulled up next to the Plymouth. He waved and got out of the car and I placed my gun on the seat." Cid frowned. The hair clinging to her forehead was still matted where a nurse had attempted to wash the blood away.

"Did he say anything?" Tally asked.

"Not at first." Cid stared at them with unblinking eyes. "Then the damn phone rang. Hell, I'd just hung up from talking with you. I thought maybe you forgot something and called back. Eleven forty-five on the nose—I checked my watch before I picked up the call. Couldn't believe my ears. Good old Victoria, saying she was at some charity auction in Atherton. She wanted to know if I'd like a coupla three-foot-tall terra cotta vases—or how does she say it—vahses, for my office. That's when Hampton tapped on my window. I told Victoria to hang on a minute, put her on hold, and hung the phone over the steering wheel. Hampton signaled for me to get out of the car, you know, like it was real important."

Tally made no comment; she simply stared at Cid in bewilderment.

"Feet hadn't even hit the ground and, bam, he wallops me across the forehead with the butt of his gun." Cid pointed to a one-inch cut that had required ten stitches to close. "I vaguely remember trying to stand and he slammed me against the car door. Next thing I knew he was dragging me toward the back of the car."

"But why did he attack you?" Tally asked.

"Couldn't figure that out myself until this morning; that's when I put it all together. Barney promised me a copy of the police report, but he never came through. After I saw Robin Stapleton and read the editorial she had written, I stopped by my house and fed Sadie. Then I met Hampton at Rudolpho's for dinner before heading out to Little Capitan for the stakeout. We agreed to touch base and share information on the case.

"At dinner, some dame, sitting across from us, had on a pair of dingle-dangly earrings. It reminded me of the conversation you and I had with Rebecca Toliver about the gold seal earrings that were missing. Naturally, I told Barney, and I also mentioned that I'd put a call into Gertrude Allendale and left a message for her to call me.

"Gertrude's a widow who's been supplementing her social security for maybe fifteen years by making jewelry. Real intricate designs. Thin gold. Always seals. I introduced Barney to her a couple of years back when he needed a gift for his daughter.

"Gertrude's not much of a phone person. She never returned my original call, so I called her again this morning. Allendale's an old bird, but she's sharp as a tack. Never forgets anything, especially names. Seems Hampton had bought a pair of earrings from her a couple of months back. Bragged about how he was going to give them to his fiancee. Barney musta realized I'd eventually figure it all out and decided to kill me." Cid looked out the window, hurt written plainly on her face.

Tally took Cid's hand in hers and held it. "Why did he put you in *your* car and not his?"

"Hell, Tal, he had a stakeout team below. He couldn't take the chance they'd find me or hear me in his car, I'd guess. And he sure as hell couldn't shoot me—they'd have heard the shots. Thank God he didn't have another scalpel in his pocket." She looked at Tally, but didn't see her. "He could have strangled me. Who knows what was going on in his mind. Probably planned on coming back to pick me up. Probably hoped I'd suffocate in the trunk . . . which, by the way, I damn near did."

"Aye, and having the stakeout team at Little Capitan was a ruse. Right?" Katie asked proudly.

"No." Tally shook her head. "Actually, he was trying to find Marsha Cox . . . and kill her. He could have blamed all of his crimes on her, including the attack on me in the hospital parking lot. And *who* in the department would have questioned him?"

Katie nodded and set her straw purse on the bed. "How did you get the other gash on your head?"

"Katie, dear, you wouldn't have a bottle of scotch in there by any chance?" Cid asked hopefully, pointing at her purse.

"If I did, Cidney, I surely wouldn't be givin' it to you. After all, a poor soul who can barely lift her head from the pillow certainly shouldn't be bendin' her elbow."

Tally looked at them both, her hand still tightly clutching Cid's. "How *did* you get the other gash?"

"He hit me again just before he put me in the trunk. Lights went out. Don't remember anything else till I heard voices. I was in such a fog. Only thing I could figure out was that Barney was coming back to kill me. That's when I recognized Cox's voice. 'Course, at the time, I didn't have a clue she was talking to a dead woman.

"Bartlett dropped by early this afternoon. Turns out Robin Stapleton was killed at her house and Cox hauled her out to Little Capitan. Who knows what Marsha thought when she saw my car, or what made her dump the body inside." Cid's eyes showed puzzlement. "And damned if I can figure out how Cox got past the stakeout team."

"I can answer that." Tally blinked and then looked directly at Cid. "After you were brought to the hospital and the doctors assured both Katie and me that you would be okay, I went back out to Little Capitan. The forensics team, Barlett, and a few uniforms were still there. Their attention was fully focused on your car and the area surrounding it. They had everything cordoned off, wouldn't let me get close. I was on my way back to my car when I remembered something Grayson had said—'Marsha may return to Little Capitan, where she controlled everything: all the elements, all the players.'" Tally felt a tingle of astonishment. "That's when I started searching the plateau. On the opposite side of the mountain, where Hampton and his stakeout team never would have seen her, I found two climbing pitons securely anchored in the granite. It's my guess, that Cox brought Robin Stapleton's dead body up the side of the mountain. The exact opposite of what she did with Cathy Dorset. And then she escaped using the same route."

Cid's voice was taut with anger. "Not possible, Tal. Police would have found the rope she used to scale the mountain."

Tally drew a breath. "No. I checked with Sarge at Great Outdoors Supply on Geary. Climbing, if you remember, is her speciality. She said Marsha would have removed the rope as she made her way back down the mountain."

Cid's voice was almost a whisper. "Another clean getaway."

"I'm just damn glad she didn't know you were in the trunk." Tally laughed. "What irony—Barney tried to kill you and ended up saving your life." Now all three women laughed.

Tally reached in the pocket of her khaki jacket and produced a pint-size bottle of sparkling cider. "The doctor said absolutely no alcohol for one week after a concussion. So this bubbly will have to do for now."

Cid's nose wrinkled. "*Cider?* Hell, it'll rust my pipes. No scotch for a week? I may as well be dead." She winked. "Katie, darlin', the glasses are in the bathroom."

Tally poured them each a small glass, and then raised hers in a toast. "To the safety of all those we love."

"And," Katie added, "may the world soon be rid of Marsha Cox."

Cid sat up gingerly, tipped her glass, and swallowed the cider in one gulp. She pointed to the table at the foot of her bed. Several helium balloons were tied to the table leg and three large bouquets of flowers obscured the top. Tally immediately spotted the single red rose nearly buried among the bouquets, and shuddered. She walked over to read the attached card. It said, "There's No Escape, My Pets."

The End

About the Author

Nancy Sanra grew up in Menlo Park, a suburb of San Francisco. A former regional sales manager, she now writes full time. She received her undergraduate degree from the University of California, and did graduate work in psychology at Columbia University.

She now makes her home in Michigan, with her life-partner Sherry, where she is currently engaged in researching and writing the third novel in the Tally McGinnis series.

Follow your dreams and always believe in the magic of love, is her Irish affirmation.

If you enjoyed *No Escape*, why not write the author and tell her so? She will be delighted to hear from you. You may send your correspondence to:

Nancy Sanra
c/o Rising Tide Press
3831 N. Oracle Rd.
Tucson, AZ 85705

Don't Miss This Exciting Mystery

DEADLY RENDEZVOUS: A Toni Underwood Mystery
Diane Davidson

Back in the lodge, Toni began wandering among the people gathered there, her eyes frantically searching for Megan. She had a frown on her face when she turned to the sergeant in charge.

"Are you positive everyone is here? All the guests? You didn't miss anybody?" Toni asked, suddenly feeling a knife-like panic rip at her insides.

"Yes, Lieutenant Underwood, this is everyone."

Toni turned to Kelly. "What villa is Mrs. Marshall in?"

"Number three, down by the pool. Here's the key."

"Let's go, Sal." Toni was already halfway out the door, with fear consuming her, enveloping her in its clutches.

The room was dark and hot. *No one's been here all night.* Toni rushed through the living room area and into the large bedroom. The bed hadn't been slept in. Megan's pink cotton robe was lying in a heap on the floor.

"Her purse and car keys are gone," Sally said quietly, seeing the fear written on Toni's face.

"Megan! Megan!" Toni called out as she headed toward the bathroom.

"Toni." Sally put her hand on Toni's arm. "Toni...she's not here," Sally said, afraid to say what she really thought.

"What do you mean she's not here? That can't be. She knew we were coming to get her today; she wouldn't leave." Fear flooded Toni's face. "Where? Where would she go, Sally?"

Then her eyes narrowed; they were like daggers, her jaw set tight. She suddenly turned without a word, and ran out of the villa and toward the lodge.

"Toni, wait! Don't do anything stupid." Sally ran after her. Catching Toni by the arm, she spun her around and forced her up against the villa wall.

"Let me go, Sal." The look in Toni's eyes was terrifying. "That bitch Clark has her hidden away somewhere as a hostage. I'm gonna kill the mother-fucker if she doesn't tell me where Megan is, right now."

"Listen to me, please," Sally pleaded.

Toni was fighting to free herself. "I don't wanna hurt you, Sal, now let me go!" Toni was screaming, as tears filled her eyes. Fear and rage filled her heart. She knew she was out of control.

"All right, god damn it, go ahead and lose it. Lose the chance of putting Nicky away for good. Lose the chance of ever finding Megan. Go ahead, you damned hothead!" Sally released her grip and stepped back.

But Toni's sobbing was breaking her heart and she softened.

"Come back inside with me," Sally gently urged. She took Toni's arm and led her toward the villa. "Let's sit down for a minute and see if we can think clearly about this, okay?"

Perspiration and tears were streaming down Toni's face; she felt sick. Her shirt was drenched with sweat, her hair stuck to her forehead.

Back in the villa, Sally turned the air-conditioning on, went into the bathroom, got a glass of water and a wet towel. "Here," she said gently, handing them to Toni.

"What are we gonna do, Sal?" Toni sounded like a lost child. It took everything Sally had not to cry.

She sat down on the bed next to Toni and put her arm around her shoulder. "We're going to get Megan back. She's not stupid, you know. I'm sure she's okay. If Clark has her stashed somewhere, we *will* get it out of her, I promise." Sally was going all out in an effort to calm and comfort Toni. "We're going to conduct ourselves like professionals. We're NOT going to let Nicky get the best of us. No matter how hard it is, you are going to hang in there. For Megan's sake, you can't fall apart. You're a police officer, the best, and that's who Nicky Clark and the rest of the department are going to see."

Toni sat on the edge of the bed staring at the floor for a long time, not moving. Finally she sighed, and looked at Sally.

"Okay, Sal, we do it your way. I'll be okay, I promise. For Megan, I'll be okay." Toni took several deep breaths, then stood, pulling her tall body up straight. "Let's find Megan." Slipping on her Raybans, she walked to the door and stepped out into the bright desert sun.

—An excerpt from *Deadly Rendezvous* ($9.99), by Diane Davidson, author of *Deadly Gamble* ($11.99).

These books are available from Rising Tide Press, and from your nearest feminist or lesbian/gay bookstore.
Please see ordering instructions.

RETURN TO ISIS
Jean Stewart
It is the year 2093, and Whit, a bold woman warrior from an Amazon nation, rescues Amelia from a dismal world where females are either breeders or drones. During their arduous journey back to the shining all-women's world of Artemis, they are unexpectedly drawn to each other. **A Lambda Literary Award Finalist** $9.99

ISIS RISING
Jean Stewart
In this stirring romantic fantasy, the familiar cast of lovable characters begin to rebuild the colony of Isis, burned to the ground ten years earlier by the dread Regulators. But evil forces threaten to destroy their dream. A swashbuckling futuristic adventure and an endearing love story all rolled into one. $11.99

WARRIORS OF ISIS
Jean Stewart
At last, the third lusty tale of high adventure and passionate romance among the Freeland Warriors. Arinna Sojourner, the evil product of genetic engineering, vows to destroy the fledgling colony of Isis with her incredible psychic powers. Whit, Kali, and other warriors battle to save their world, in this novel bursting with life, love, heroines and villains. $11.99

EMERALD CITY BLUES
Jean Stewart
When the comfortable yuppie world of Chris Olson and Jennifer Hart collides with the desperate lives of Reb and Flynn, two lesbian runaways struggling to survive on the streets of Seattle, the forecast is trouble. A gritty, enormously readable novel of contemporary lesbigay life which raises real questions about the meaning of family and community, and about the walls we construct. A celebration of the healing powers of love. $11.99

ROUGH JUSTICE
Claire Youmans
When Glenn Lowry's sunken fishing boat turns up four years after his disappearance, foul play is suspected. Classy, ambitious Prosecutor Janet Schilling immediately launches a murder investigation which produces several surprising suspects—one of them her own former lover Catherine Adams, now living a reclusive life on an island. A real page-turner! $10.99

FEATHERING YOUR NEST: An Interactive Workbook & Guide to a Loving Lesbian Relationship
Gwen Leonhard, M.ED./Jennie Mast, MSW
This fresh, insightful guide and workbook for lesbian couples provides effective ways to build and nourish your relationships. Includes fun exercises & creative ways to spark romance, solve conflict, fight fair, conquer boredom, spice up your sex lives & enjoy life together. Plus much more. $14.99

AND LOVE CAME CALLING
Beverly Shearer

The rough and ready days of the Old West come alive with the timeless story of love between two women: Kenny Smith, a stage coach driver in Jackson, Colorado and Sophie McLaren, a young woman forced to marry, then widowed. The women meet after Kenny is shot by bandits during a stage coach holdup. And love blooms when Sophie finds herself the unexpected rescuer of the good-looking wounded driver. $11.99

CORNERS OF THE HEART
Leslie Grey

A captivating novel of love and suspense in which beautiful French-born Chris Benet and English professor Katya Michaels meet and fall in love. But their budding love is shadowed by a vicious killer, whom they must outwit. Your heart will pound as the story races to its heart-stopping conclusion. $9.95

DANGER IN HIGH PLACES
Sharon Gilligan

Set against the backdrop of Washington, D.C., this riveting mystery introduces freelance photographer and amateur sleuth, Alix Nicholson. Alix stumbles on a deadly scheme, and with the help of a lesbian congressional aide, unravels the mystery. $9.99

DANGER! CROSS CURRENTS
Sharon Gilligan

The exciting sequel to *Danger in High Places* brings freelance photographer Alix Nicholson face-to-face with an old love and a murder. When Alix's landlady turns up dead, and her much younger lover, Leah Claire, is the prime suspect, Alix launches a frantic campaign to find the real killer. $9.99

PLAYING FOR KEEPS
Stevie Rios

In this sparkling tale of love and adventure, Lindsay West, a musician, travels to Caracas, where she meets three people who change her life forever: Rob Heron a gay man, who becomes her dearest friend; Her lover Mercedes Luego, who takes Lindsay on a life-altering adventure down the Amazon River; And the mysterious jungle-dwelling woman Arminta, who touches their souls $10.99

NIGHTSHADE
Karen Williams

Alex Spherris finds herself the new owner of a magical bell, which some people would kill for. With this bell, she is ushered into a strange & wonderful world and meets Orielle, who melts her frozen heart. A heartwarming romance spun in the best tradition of storytelling. $11.99

DREAMCATCHER
Lori Byrd

This timeless story of love and friendship introduces Sunny Calhoun, a college student, who falls in love with Eve Phillips, a literary agent. A richly woven novel capturing the wonder and pain of love between a younger and an older woman. $9.99

AGENDA FOR MURDER
Joan Albarella
Though haunted by memories of love and loss from her years of service in Viet Nam, Nikki Barnes is finally putting back the pieces of her life, and learning to feel again. But she quickly realizes that the college where she teaches is no haven from violence and death, as she comes face to face with murder and betrayal in this least likely of all places—her college campus.   [Avail.11/98] $11.99

HEARTSTONE AND SABER
Jacqui Singleton
You can almost hear the sabers clash in this rousing tale of good and evil, of passionate love between a bold warrior queen and a beautiful healer with magical powers. $10.99

SHADOWS AFTER DARK
Ouida Crozier
Fans of vampire erotica will adore this! When wings of death spread over Kyril's home world, she is sent to Earth on a mission—find a cure for the deadly disease. Once here, she meets and falls in love with Kathryn, who is enthralled yet horrified to learn that her mysterious, darkly exotic lover is...a vampire. This tender, beautifully written love story is the ultimate lesbian vampire novel! $9.95

TROPICAL STORM
Linda Kay Silva
Another winning, action-packed adventure/romance featuring smart and sassy heroines, an exotic jungle setting, and a plot with more twists and turns than a coiled cobra. Megan has disappeared into the Costa Rican rain forest and it's up to Delta and Connie to find her. Can they reach Megan before it's too late? Will Storm risk everything to save the woman she loves? Fast-paced, full of wonderful characters and surprises. Not to be missed. $11.99

SWEET BITTER LOVE
Rita Schiano
Susan Fredrickson is a woman of fire and ice—a successful high-powered executive, she is by turns sexy and aloof. And from the moment writer Jenny Ceretti spots her at the Village Coffeehouse, her serene life begins to change. As their friendship explodes into a blazing love affair, Jenny discovers that all is not as it appears, while Susan is haunted by ghosts from her past. Schiano serves up passion and drama in this roller-coaster romance. $10.99

SIDE DISH
Kim Taylor
She's funny, she's attractive, she's lovable—and she doesn't know it. Meet Muriel, aka Mutt, a twenty-something wayward waitress with a college degree, who has resigned herself to low standards, simple pleasures, and erotic fantasies. Though seeming to get by on margaritas and old movies, in her heart of hearts, Mutt is actually searching for true love. While Mutt chases the bars with her best friend, Jeff, she is, in turn, chased by Diane, a former college classmate with a decidedly romantic agenda. When a rich, seductive Beverly Hills lawyer named Allison steals Mutt's heart, she is in for trouble, and like the glamorous facade of Sunset Boulevard, things are not quite as they seem. A delightfully funny read. $11.99

NO WITNESSES
Nancy Sanra
This cliff-hanger of a mystery set in San Francisco, introduces Detective Tally McGinnis, whose ex-lover Pamela Tresdale is arrested for the grisly murder of a wealthy Texas heiress. Tally rushes to the rescue despite friends' warnings, and is drawn once again into Pamela's web of deception and betrayal as she attempts to clear her and find the real killer. $9.99

NO ESCAPE
Nancy Sanra
This edgy, fast-paced sequel to *No Witnesses*, also set in picturesque San Francisco, is a story of drugs, love and jealousy. Late one rain-drenched night, nurse Melinda Morgan is found murdered. Who cut her life short, plunging a scalpel into her heart, then disappeared into the night? As lesbian PI Tally McGinnis sorts through the bizarre evidence, she can almost sense the diabolical Marsha Cox lurking in the shadows. You will be shocked by the secrets behind the gruesome murder. $11.99

DEADLY RENDEZVOUS
Diane Davidson
A string of brutal murders in the middle of the desert plunges Lieutenant Toni Underwood and her lover Megan into a high profile investigation which uncovers a world of drugs, corruption and murder, as well as the dark side of the human mind. An explosive, fast-paced, action-packed whodunit. $9.99

DEADLY GAMBLE
Diane Davidson
Former police detective Toni Underwood is catapulted back into the world of crime by a mysterious letter from her favorite aunt. Black sheep of the family and a prominent madam, Vera Valentine fears she is about to be murdered—a distinct possibility, given her underworld connections. With the help of onetime partner (and possibly future lover) Sergeant Sally Murphy, Toni takes on the seamy, ruthless underbelly of Las Vegas, where appearance and reality are often at odds. Flamboyant characters and unsavory thugs make for a cast of likely suspects... and keep the reader guessing until the last page. $11.99

CLOUD NINE AFFAIR
Katherine E. Kreuter
Chris Grandy—rebellious, wealthy, twenty-something—has disappeared in India, along with her hippie lover Monica Ward. Desperate to bring her home, Christine's millionaire father hires expert Paige Taylor. But the trail to Christine is mined with obstacles, as powerful enemies plot to eliminate her. A witty, sophisticated & entertaining mystery. $11.99

COMING ATTRACTIONS
Bobbi D. Marolt
It's been three years since she's made love to a woman; three years that she's buried herself in work as a successful columnist for one of New York's top newspapers. Helen Townsend admits, at last, she's tired of being lonely....and of being closeted. Enter Princess Charming in the shapely form of Cory Chamberlain, a gifted concert pianist. And Helen embraces joy once again. But can two lovers find happiness when one yearns to break out of the closet and breathe free, while the other fears that will destroy her career? A sunny blend of humor, heart and passion. A novel which captures the bliss and blunderings of love. $11.99

HOW TO ORDER

TITLE   AUTHOR   PRICE

- ❑ **Agenda for Murder**-Joan Albarella 11.99
- ❑ **And Love Came Calling**-Beverly Shearer 11.99
- ❑ **Cloud 9 Affair**-Katherine Kreuter 11.99
- ❑ **Coming Attractions**-Bobbi Marolt 11.99
- ❑ **Corners of the Heart**-Leslie Grey 9.95
- ❑ **Danger! Cross Currents**-Sharon Gilligan 9.99
- ❑ **Danger in High Places**-Sharon Gilligan 9.95
- ❑ **Deadly Gamble**-Diane Davidson 11.99
- ❑ **Deadly Rendezvous**-Diane Davidson 9.99
- ❑ **Dreamcatcher**-Lori Byrd 9.99
- ❑ **Emerald City Blues**-Jean Stewart 11.99
- ❑ **Feathering Your Nest**-Gwen Leonhard/ Jennie Mast 14.99
- ❑ **Heartstone and Saber**-Jacqui Singleton 10.99
- ❑ **Isis Rising**-Jean Stewart 11.99
- ❑ **Nightshade**-Karen Williams 11.99
- ❑ **No Escape**-Nancy Sanra 11.99
- ❑ **No Witnesses**-Nancy Sanra 9.99
- ❑ **Playing for Keeps**-Stevie Rios 10.99
- ❑ **Return to Isis**-Jean Stewart 9.99
- ❑ **Rough Justice**-Claire Youmans 10.99
- ❑ **Shadows After Dark**-Ouida Crozier 9.99
- ❑ **Side Dish**-Kim Taylor 11.99
- ❑ **Sweet Bitter Love**-Rita Schiano 10.99
- ❑ **Tropical Storm**-Linda Kay Silva 11.99
- ❑ **Warriors of Isis**-Jean Stewart 11.99

Please send me the books I have checked. I enclose a check or money order (not cash), plus $3 for the first book and $1 for each additional book to cover shipping and handling. Or bill my ❑Visa/Mastercard ❑American Express.

Or call our Toll Free Number 1-800-648-5333 if using a credit card.
CARD # _____ EXP.DATE_____

NAME (PLEASE PRINT) _____SIGNTURE_____

ADDRESS _____

CITY_____

STATE_____ZIP_____
❑ Arizona residents add 7% tax to total.

RISING TIDE PRESS, 3831 N. ORACLE RD., TUCSON AZ 85705